"Chelsea, what's going on?"

Johnny clutched his cell phone to his ear and at the same time sat up and turned on the lamp on his nightstand.

"That man—that man is here. He's tried to b-break in." The words came from her amid sobs. "He—he was at my back d-door and breaking the gl-glass to get in."

"Hang up and call Lane," he instructed as he got out of bed.

"I...already called, but n-nobody is here yet."

Johnny could hear the abject terror in her voice, and an icy fear shot through him. "Where are you now?"

"I'm in the kitchen."

"Get to the bathroom and lock yourself in. Do you hear me? Lock yourself in the bathroom and I'll be there as quickly as I can," he instructed.

"Please hurry. I don't know where he is now and I'm so scared."

"Just get to the bathroom. Lock the door and don't open it for anyone but me or the police."

CLOSING IN ON THE COWBOY

New York Times Bestselling Author
CARLA CASSIDY

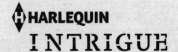

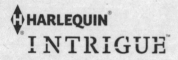

ISBN-13: 978-1-335-58201-0

Closing in on the Cowboy

Copyright © 2022 by Carla Bracale

Recycling programs
for this product may
not exist in your area.

Harlequin Enterprises ULC
22 Adelaide St. West, 41st Floor
Toronto, Ontario M5H 4E3, Canada
www.Harlequin.com

Printed in U.S.A.

Carla Cassidy is an award-winning, *New York Times* bestselling author who has written over 170 books, including 150 for Harlequin. She has won the Centennial Award from Romance Writers of America. Most recently she won the 2019 Write Touch Readers Award for her Harlequin Intrigue title *Desperate Strangers*. Carla believes the only thing better than curling up with a good book is sitting down at the computer with a good story to write.

Books by Carla Cassidy

Harlequin Intrigue

Kings of Coyote Creek

Closing in on the Cowboy

Desperate Strangers
Desperate Intentions
Desperate Measures
Stalked in the Night
Stalker in the Shadows

Scene of the Crime

Scene of the Crime: Bridgewater, Texas
Scene of the Crime: Bachelor Moon
Scene of the Crime: Widow Creek
Scene of the Crime: Mystic Lake
Scene of the Crime: Black Creek
Scene of the Crime: Deadman's Bluff
Scene of the Crime: Return to Bachelor Moon
Scene of the Crime: Return to Mystic Lake
Scene of the Crime: Baton Rouge
Scene of the Crime: Killer Cove
Scene of the Crime: Who Killed Shelly Sinclair?
Scene of the Crime: Means and Motive

Visit the Author Profile page at Harlequin.com.

CAST OF CHARACTERS

Johnny King—When his father is murdered, he vows vengeance, but first he'll have to deal with the return of the woman he once loved.

Chelsea Black—When she returns to the small town of Coyote Creek after five years in New York City, she quickly realizes she's in danger from an unknown assailant and that she also must face the man she walked away from.

Leroy Hicks—A former King ranch hand. Did he kill big John King and is he now the man tormenting Chelsea?

Tanya Brooks—Does the attractive woman want to kill Chelsea because of romantic jealousy?

Adam Pearson—Does he harbor a secret obsession for Chelsea, an obsession that has grown into a killing rage?

Jerry Walkins—Has Chelsea's superfan followed her from New York with murder in his mind?

Caleb King—Has Johnny's youngest brother killed his father in a fit of anger?

Chapter One

Johnny King breathed deeply of the fresh spring scent of the pasture. The grass had turned to green once again, and all the trees were sporting new leaves after a long, cold winter.

The April afternoon sun was warm on his shoulders as he leisurely rode his horse along the fence line that separated the King property from the Blacks' ranch.

There was nothing he loved more than checking on the huge herd of cattle that had made the King ranch one of the most successful in the entire state of Kansas.

Normally his father would be riding alongside him, but the sudden death of the man who had been mayor had warranted a special election, and Big John King had thrown his hat into the ring. The election was due to take place in five weeks, and so right now all of his father's time and energy was being spent trying to get the lead against the two other men running for the office.

As far as Johnny was concerned, his father was the sure winner. John King was a powerhouse businessman who not only ran the very successful cattle business but also had financial interests in half the stores in town. Beyond that, he was a humble man, who was well-liked and respected in the small Kansas town of Coyote Creek.

Johnny now emptied his head of all thoughts of his father and the election and urged his horse, Lady, to go faster. He always liked a swift run along the fence line from a tall, thick oak tree in the pasture to an old, abandoned wagon on the Black property in the distance. He gave Lady free rein to run while he lowered his head to make sure his black cowboy hat stayed put on his head.

It was only as he approached the old wagon that he reined her in and slowed to a walk. It was also only as he came closer to the wagon that he saw a pair of long, shapely feminine legs poking out of the wagon and propped up with bare feet on the edge of the wooden bench seat.

They were sexy legs that he instantly recognized. Chelsea. He barely had time to process that she was here in front of him when she sat up and her unusual, nearly neon-green eyes widened in surprise. "Johnny," she said.

"Chelsea, I...I didn't know you were back in town." He steeled himself for the rush of emotions that raged through him at the unexpected sight of her.

It helped somewhat that she didn't look quite the same as she had five years before when she'd left here for a new life in New York City. At that time, she'd left Coyote Creek with a headful of dreams and his raw, hurting heart.

"I've been back for about a week now, but I've been sticking pretty close to home."

"On vacation?" he asked.

She shook her head. Her pale blond hair sparkled in the sunshine as she gazed at him soberly. "I'm back home to stay." She looked at someplace in the distance.

He was surprised, and yet he wasn't. Her fall from grace as a top model had been very public and covered by tabloids and a variety of news media.

In her first year in New York, she had been discovered and proclaimed the new It Girl in the runway modeling world. Her long hair had been cut off for a short, edgy cut that emphasized her large eyes and high cheekbones.

She'd always been slender, but now clad in a pair of jean shorts and a tight navy blue T-shirt, she looked far too thin and fragile. Once again, he fought against a surge of unwanted emotions.

He never wanted to care about her again. There had been a time when he'd been crazy-mad in love with her. He'd wanted to marry her and have babies with her. He'd dreamed of the life they would build here, and he'd believed she shared in those dreams.

She'd destroyed his love for her when she'd given him back his engagement ring and had basically told him he just wasn't enough for her. There was no way his heart would ever be open to her again.

"Did Melinda come home with you as well?" he asked. When Chelsea had left for New York, her best friend Melinda Wells had gone along with her.

"Yes, Melinda came home with me," she replied.

"So, you're staying with your mother?" he asked. She nodded positively. "I'm sure she's glad to have you back home."

Chelsea released a small, dry laugh. "You know Stella. It's hard to know from moment to moment how she feels. One minute she's happy I'm home, and the next she's telling me what a big loser I am."

He winced. He knew Stella Black could be extremely mean-spirited behind closed doors while being a pillar of society in Coyote Creek. "I'm sorry if she's giving you a hard time," he replied.

Chelsea shrugged. "I'm used to it. So, how have you been?"

There were so many things he wanted to say to her. He wanted to tell her how deeply she'd hurt him when she'd broken off their engagement. He wanted her to know that it had taken him a very long time to get over that pain and the absence of her in his life.

More importantly he wanted to ask her if leaving him and all the love he'd had to offer her had really been worth it. Had she thought about him at all after she'd left? Had she missed him at all?

And yet he didn't want to know. Nor did he want to reveal to her the depth of his pain when she had left him. "Things are good. Lately I've been staying really busy here at the ranch with my dad otherwise occupied."

"I heard he was running for mayor." She laid the book she held in her hand to the side and sat up straighter. A light breeze blew a fragrance of lilacs and vanilla to him. It was a familiar scent, one that she had always worn, and one that had always stirred a wealth of desire inside him.

"Yeah. He's deep in the campaigning right now," Johnny replied, trying to ignore how her scent still had the ability to affect him.

"How's your mother?"

"She's been through the wringer, but finally the cancer is behind her, and she's looking forward to the future."

"She had cancer?" Chelsea appeared stricken.

"Breast cancer, twice. She's undergone radiation, chemo and finally a double mastectomy. She's still a bit fragile, but she's doing okay and taking it one day at a time."

"Please tell her I asked about her," she said, a touch of sadness in her voice. At one time Chelsea and Johnny's mother, Margaret, had been very close.

Of course, that had all changed when Chelsea had called off the engagement and left town.

"I'll tell her." He shifted positions in the saddle. "So, what are your plans now that you're back in town?"

"My only plan at the moment is to move out of my mother's house and into someplace else as soon as possible. Other than that, I don't know what comes next for me. I'm just taking some time for myself right now." Her eyes darkened with what appeared to be haunted shadows.

An awkward silence grew between them. For him it held the weight of a thousand words unsaid… and a hundred questions he wanted to ask her but wouldn't.

"How's your brother?" he finally asked.

A quick smile curved her lips. "Jacob is good. I'm hoping he's planning on moving back here soon."

"Is he still a policeman?"

"Yeah, he's still on the Kansas City police force. I'm trying to talk him into applying for a position in the police department here."

Chelsea's brother was thirty-four, five years older than Johnny and eight years older than Chelsea. He'd left Coyote Creek soon after graduating from high school and hadn't been back since.

"I'm sure he'd make a good addition to our police force," Johnny said. "Well, I'd better get moving. I guess I'll see you around town." He pulled the reins to turn away.

"Johnny…"

He turned around to face her once again. Before she could speak again a gunshot boomed. Immediately a scream rent the air. Every nerve and muscle in Johnny's body tensed. He knew that scream. It was his mother. Another gunshot cracked, and the screaming continued.

Johnny whirled Lady around and took off galloping toward the house. His heart beat frantically, and the taste of fear filled his mouth. Who had shot a gun, and why was his mother screaming? Had she somehow accidentally been shot?

As the large ranch house came into view, horror swept through him at the scene of utter chaos. His mother stood in the middle of the driveway, with Johnny's younger brother Luke obviously trying to move her toward the safety of the house.

His sister, Ashley was just stepping out of the front door. "Ashley, stay inside," Johnny yelled as he dismounted his horse and pulled his gun from his holster. He hit the ground. Thankfully, Luke managed to get their mother into the house, although Johnny could still hear her hysterical sobs.

Now he saw why she had screamed. Big John King lay sprawled on his back in the driveway between the house and the garage. Johnny began to crawl on the ground toward his father, unsure if more bullets would fly.

"Hang on, Dad. I'm coming," he yelled. He crawled as fast as he could go, scared out of his mind because his dad hadn't moved or responded to him in any way.

What had happened here? Who had shot his father, and how badly was he wounded? A million thoughts raced through his head in the moments it took him to reach his father's side.

His father was vibrant and bigger than life. He had always seemed invincible. He was the head of the family, the man in charge of keeping the King ranch one of the most profitable ranches in a four-state area. He was the man who had taught Johnny everything he knew.

But when Johnny reached his father's side, his horror only increased. Big John's chest was covered in blood. "Dad...Dad!" Johnny cried out. He pressed his hands on the bleeding wound, not knowing what else to do.

"Johnny," Luke yelled to him from the house.

"Call 9-1-1. We need an ambulance and the sheriff right away," Johnny yelled back.

"Already done," Luke replied.

"Just hang on, Dad. I'm right here with you." Johnny grabbed his father's hand and squeezed it tightly. "Do you hear me, Dad? I'm right here."

The sound of a siren filled the air. It should have

given Johnny an enormous sense of relief, but it didn't. He already knew it was too late. A sharp pang of grief pierced through him, along with an overwhelming sense of rage.

His father was dead. Big John King had been murdered by somebody, and Johnny wouldn't stop until he found the person responsible.

THE MURDER OF cattle baron John King was the biggest scandal to hit the small town of Coyote Creek since Annie Harris had shot her husband in the butt while he was making love to his mistress in their marital bed.

As Chelsea Black dressed to attend the funeral for John, her head was filled with myriad thoughts and emotions. This was the first time she would be making an appearance in public since returning home.

If she knew the people of this small town as well as she thought she did, then most of them would know about her skyrocket climb to fame in the modeling world in New York…and her disastrous fall in disgrace.

There was a part of her that would like to skip the funeral and remain hidden away from everyone here in her childhood bedroom. But there was a much bigger part of her that wanted—that needed—to be there the way the King family had always been there for her over the years. Her need to pay her respects outweighed the knowledge that she would be fodder for the gossipers in town.

John King had shown her the kind of paternal love she'd never had since her father hadn't stuck around to raise her and had been completely absent from her life.

Margaret had known that Stella could be a harsh, critical mother to Chelsea, and while Margaret had never said a single word against her mother, Margaret had always been warm and loving and supportive of Chelsea.

Chelsea had become friends with Ashley and Luke King. She'd found the youngest King sibling, Caleb, to be a strange kid who had grown into a strange adult.

And then there was Johnny. She'd fallen in love with him when she was thirteen years old and he was sixteen. It was when she was sixteen that he'd told her he was crazy about her too, but he wouldn't date her or have any real relationship with her until she turned eighteen.

Still, they had spent many stolen hours together just talking every day after school or when he was finished doing his daily chores on the ranch. When she was eighteen, they had officially begun to date.

She released a deep sigh as she pulled on the only black dress she had in her closet. Seeing Johnny again had stirred all kinds of emotions…ones she'd tried to forget over the last five years.

It didn't matter what she might still feel where Johnny was concerned. She knew she'd hurt him terribly when she'd broken off their engagement and had left town. He'd probably spent the last five years hating her for what she had done to him.

"Chelsea, are you about ready to go?" Chelsea's mother knocked rapidly on the bedroom door. "We don't want to be late."

Chelsea gave a last look in her dresser mirror and then opened her door. "I'm ready."

Stella Black was a very attractive woman. Although she was only fifty-eight years old, her blond hair had turned a beautiful silver shade that was a perfect foil to her blue-green eyes.

Those eyes now gazed at Chelsea from head to toe, and her upper lip slowly curled up. Chelsea steeled herself. The upper-lip curl was never a good sign.

"That dress is far too short and tight. It might have been appropriate in New York City, but it's absolutely not appropriate for Coyote Creek. And I can't believe you allowed somebody to cut your hair into that choppy, ridiculous style."

"Are you finished?" Chelsea asked with a sigh. "This is the only black dress I own. Besides, everyone in town will have something to say about what I wear and how I look. After all, I was a top model who ruined my career with drugs and also had a variety of undiagnosed mental illness issues."

A wealth of bitterness rose up in the back of her throat. The tabloids had been brutal to her, as had the people who were supposed to have had her back. The only person who had tried to clean up the bad press with the truth had been Melinda. Chelsea's best friend since third grade, Melinda had worked as Chelsea's secretary and press person after she had begun her successful modeling journey.

"Don't even bring that up to me," her mother replied curtly. "I can't wait for your brother to move back here. He has never given me any trouble." She released an audible, disapproving sigh. "Let's just go. I told you I don't want to be late."

Minutes later Stella was behind the wheel of the car, and Chelsea sat in the passenger seat as they headed toward the Coyote Creek Cemetery.

Nerves fluttered through Chelsea. This would be her first public outing since she'd arrived home and she couldn't believe it was to John's funeral. Who had killed him? So far, according to all the news sources she'd seen and heard, there didn't seem to be any leads in the case.

She could almost feel sorry for police chief Lane Caldwell. The pressure on him to solve the murder would be huge. Not only from a lot of people in town but also from the influential King family and their equally influential friends as well.

As they drew closer to the cemetery, thoughts of Johnny filled her head once again. She hadn't seen him again since the day of the murder, but she knew Big John's death had assuredly shattered him.

Johnny had always idolized his father, and as he'd gotten older the two had been not only father and son but best friends as well. She couldn't think of anything that might have changed that close relationship in the past five years.

She knew Johnny would not only be heartbroken about his father's death but also filled with a burning desire to find the guilty party.

If she had made a different decision years ago, then she would have been by Johnny's side today. She would have held him tightly as he grieved. She would have loved him through the trauma.

Who would be holding him tonight when the funeral was over and all the people went home? For all she knew, he was married and had a family by now. She couldn't begrudge him that. She hoped he had found love after she'd left him. It didn't matter that the very idea of him with another woman tugged at her heart more than a little bit.

The cemetery parking lot was full, and an attendant guided Stella to a spot in a grassy area among dozens of other cars. "This will be the biggest social event we've seen here in Coyote Creek in years," Stella said as she shut off the car engine. "Everybody who is anybody will be here."

Chelsea bit her tongue. She certainly didn't view a funeral as a social event. But her mother saw every outing as an opportunity to remind people that she, as president of the Ladies' League and a friend of City Hall, was a powerful woman who should be respected and revered.

As the two women got out of the car and headed toward the crowd gathered in and around a large white tent, Chelsea steeled herself for the scrutiny that would be on her, a scrutiny she hoped wouldn't detract from the King family and the solemn ceremony that had brought everyone together.

Rather than stand at the back of the crowd, her mother grabbed her arm and wove her way around people until they were beneath the tent. Chelsea would have much preferred to stand at the back as she was aware of the stares and whispers that followed in her wake. But when she tried to pull away from Stella, she merely tightened her grip on Chelsea's arm.

The King family stood together and appeared to make a protective circle around frail-looking Margaret…except for Johnny. He stood slightly separate from the others. His features were expressionless, except for his blue eyes. They simmered with what appeared to be a combination of both deep grief and rich rage.

Why did he not have anyone standing next to him…a wife or a girlfriend, supporting him through this dark time? He looked stoic and so all alone.

Despite the time that had gone by, her heart ached for him.

His gaze suddenly caught hers. For several long moments their gazes remained locked, and in the depths of his eyes she thought she saw a whisper of the man who had once loved her. There was a softness there only for a minute, and then it was gone, making her wonder if she'd only imagined it.

At that time Pastor Jim Jeffries began the eulogy. The graveside service was fairly short, and afterward Stella insisted they go to the King ranch to show their support as intimate friends of the family.

By that time all Chelsea wanted was to go back home and hide in her room. She'd had enough of the whispering, the raised brows and furtive glances she knew she'd garnered.

She'd tugged at the hemline of her dress, wishing for another inch or two in length as she'd kept her gaze mostly focused on the ground or on the trees in the distance. And now she would be in a smaller group of people at the King ranch.

She hoped Melinda would be at the ranch. She'd seen her friend at the funeral, but the two had been too far apart to speak to each other. In fact, Chelsea hadn't spoken to Melinda since the two of them had come back home.

As Stella drove up to the King house, Chelsea regarded it curiously. She was oddly pleased that it still looked like it had five years ago. It was an impressive place, a huge rambling ranch with a wrap-around porch.

Chelsea knew there were seven bedrooms, five bathrooms and a formal dining room along with a huge great room and kitchen. It was the biggest house in Coyote Creek and decorated beautifully.

Yet despite its beauty, there was a warmth inside that instantly made people feel welcome. This had been Chelsea's home away from home when she'd been growing up, and there were many happy memories within its walls.

Stella parked, and together the two got out of the car and headed for the front door. They were greeted there by Robert Martin, fellow rancher and good friend of the King family.

"Robert," Stella said, and the two of them briefly hugged.

"Chelsea, it's nice to see you back in town," Robert said. "Although with this mess, it's a terrible time to be here."

Robert was in his midsixties. He was a tall, slightly burly man with a gentle smile. He'd been a widower for years, and Chelsea had always believed he had a secret crush on her mother. In any case, he'd always been kind to Chelsea.

"Thank you, Robert," she replied.

He looked back at Stella. "The family isn't back here yet, but there are several others in the great room and kitchen."

"Then we'll just head in there," Stella replied.

In the kitchen several women bustled around setting up trays of food to carry to the dining-room table. Stella began to help them while she waved Chelsea to a chair in the corner of the kitchen. Chelsea would have insisted on helping but knew she would only get in the other women's way.

Minutes later the King family arrived home. Chelsea got up and walked into the great room where Margaret was seated in one of the cranberry wing-backed chairs. Johnny stood on one side of her and Luke on the other, two sober-faced sentries of protection.

Chelsea's only desire at the moment was to offer support and love to the woman who had been like a second mom to her. However, she wasn't sure how Margaret would receive her. After all, Chelsea was the woman who had broken her son's heart five years before.

Before Chelsea got all the way to her, Margaret stood and opened her arms to her. Unexpected tears blurred Chelsea's vision as she felt Margaret's arms surrounding her. The tears became soft sobs as the two women hugged long and hard. Margaret had always been a small woman, but now she felt achingly fragile.

"Margaret, I'm so sorry for your loss," Chelsea managed to get out between sobs as the two finally separated. "I can't even believe this has happened."

Margaret's lower lip trembled. "None of us can believe this has happened. But it's so good to see you again, Chelsea. You need to come over and eat some of my cheddar mashed potatoes and put a little meat on your bones." She offered Chelsea a small, sad smile. "You always loved my mashed potatoes."

Chelsea quickly swiped at her tears and returned Margaret's smile. "Yes, I did, and you know I've always loved you."

At that moment several other people descended on Margaret, and Chelsea moved away. Aware of more stares and whispers following her, she stepped outside and walked around the porch to the side of the house where there were two wicker chairs with a small glass-topped table between them.

She sank down in one of the chairs and tried to get hold of her emotions. She hadn't meant to cry, but seeing Margaret again, knowing how much the older woman had loved and adored her husband, had nearly undone Chelsea.

She closed her eyes and raised her face to the warm sun. She had no idea how long Stella intended to stay, but Chelsea was ready to go home. She'd paid her respects to Margaret, and that was all that was important.

She wasn't sure how long she'd sat there before she sensed somebody nearby. She opened her eyes to see Johnny standing at the porch railing with his back toward her.

"Johnny," she said softly. He turned to look at her. His eyes were dark and unfathomable, and his features were taut with tension. "Johnny…I'm so sorry about your dad."

He gave a curt nod of his head.

"Does the sheriff have any clues as to who might have done this?" she asked.

He released a deep sigh. "Not yet, but sooner or later we'll catch the person responsible." His eyes flashed with anger. "And whoever it is, he better hope the sheriff gets to him before I do." His hands tightened into fists at his sides and then relaxed. "I'm rather surprised to see you here."

"Why wouldn't I be here? You know how much I always loved your family…how much I loved your father." Her voice broke as she once again found herself swallowing against the deep emotion that threatened to overwhelm her.

It was an emotion not only wrought from the death of Big John but also from the regrets that filled her heart with a heaviness, the regret of losing five years here.

"So, how are you all getting along?" she asked.

He shoved his hands in his suit-pants pockets and shrugged. "It depends on what time you ask. Mom is alternating between trying to stay strong and completely falling apart. Luke is quieter than I've ever seen him, and Ashley is stifling her own grief in an effort to be strong for Mom. As for Caleb…who knows how he's dealing? He hasn't been around much since the murder."

"I'm just so sorry, Johnny," she said again.

"Thanks." Again, their gazes met and held for several long moments, and in the blue depths of his eyes she once again thought she saw a softness.

She'd always thought Johnny was one of the handsomest men in town, and the past five years hadn't changed that. His black, shiny hair was on the shaggy side, but that didn't detract from his strong, bold features or the sapphire shine of his eyes.

Now, she believed that he at almost thirty years old was even more handsome than he'd been at twenty-five. There was a new maturity to his features that only made him more attractive.

The black suit he wore only enhanced his attractiveness, the jacket fitting perfectly on his big, broad shoulders, and the trousers hanging nicely on his long, muscular legs.

There had always been a spark with him, a heady pull toward him, and she was surprised to realize the spark was still there for her. In this moment she couldn't believe she'd turned her back and walked away from this man and the love she'd known he'd had for her.

"So, what happens now for all of you?" she asked.

"Nothing much changes except I'll be running the ranch instead of my father. Actually, Dad left meticulous instructions in the event that anything happened to him. So, Luke and I will continue to work here."

"What about Ashley and Caleb? What are they up to these days?" She hesitated a moment and then continued. "I'm sorry if I'm asking too many questions. I'm just trying to play catch-up, but maybe this isn't the time or place to do that."

"You're fine," he replied. "Ashley now owns a trinket-and-dress shop in town, and Caleb...well, nobody is ever sure what he's doing. He's still into painting, but nobody has seen any of his work."

"Are you all still living here?" Once again there were so many things she wanted to say to him, but now definitely wasn't the time or place for those kinds of things. There might never be a time for her to speak her heart to him.

"After doing a bunch of renovations, I'm now living in the foreman's cabin. Luke has built a house on the property down by the old pond. Ashley has a house in town but has moved back in here temporarily, and Caleb still lives here."

"What kind of renovations have you done to the foreman's cabin?" Oh, how well she remembered that place! Many times in the past the two of them had met there to spend intimate, alone time together. Just thinking about those passionate trysts evoked a sweet heat to rush through her. Was he remembering those moments too?

"I completely gutted the place except for the fireplace. The kitchen is now updated, and I added a second bedroom," he said.

"Oh, that sounds nice." Once again, their gazes met each other's and held for a long, breathless moment. Was it possible there might be a chance that he'd forgive her for what she had done to him in the past? Was it possible they could reignite the love they had once had for each other and share a beautiful future together?

"Darling…there you are." An attractive brunette rounded the corner and moved to Johnny's side, dousing any hope Chelsea might have momentarily entertained about a future with Johnny.

Chapter Two

It was a beautiful Tuesday morning when Johnny and Luke got into Johnny's truck and headed away from the King ranch. "I can't believe everything is greening up and blooming already," Luke said.

"Yeah, let's just hope the spring storms stay away from us," Johnny replied.

"They rarely do," Luke replied.

"Then let's just hope if the storms find us, they aren't too bad this year." Johnny glanced over at his brother. Luke had been unusually quiet since their father's murder. In fact, he'd been quiet and yet he'd also been negative, which wasn't like him at all.

The two fell silent for the remainder of the fifteen-minute drive to Coyote Creek proper. Although the town was small, it had a thriving downtown. Along Main Street there was a two-block run of businesses that were kept healthy by the support of the town's people.

Johnny once again glanced at his brother. With only a year between them, the two brothers were very close, although there had been a lot of competitiveness when they were growing up. Luke had always been content just being a ranch hand, but Johnny was hoping he'd step up now and take on more responsibility.

However, ranch business wasn't what had brought the two into town today. The funeral had been two days ago, and chief of police Lane Caldwell hadn't come to see them with any updates on the investigation since a couple of days before the funeral. And what they all wanted, what they all needed right now was answers as to who had committed the murder.

The Coyote Creek Police Station was in a long brick building. The building held not only Lane's and his men's offices but on one side was a tattoo shop and on the other side was his sister's store. Her store was closed for now, but he knew eventually she'd need to get back to her real life.

Actually, they were all going to have to find a new normal. His father's death had changed and would change things in ways he had yet to even consider.

He shoved everything out of his mind as he pulled into a parking space in front of the station and turned off his engine.

"Let's do it," Luke said.

Together the two of them got out of the truck. Johnny pushed open the police-station door with Luke at his heels. Henrietta Benson sat behind the reception desk, where she had sat for as long as Johnny could remember.

"Good morning, Henrietta," Johnny said.

"Johnny, Luke." She greeted them with a smile.

"Hi, Henrietta. Is he in?" Johnny asked.

"He is." She pushed a button that unlocked the door between the public and the officers. Johnny and Luke entered a long hallway. Lane's office was the first doorway on the right.

As they walked in, Lane looked up from whatever he'd been reading, and his eyes widened. He half stood, but Johnny waved him back down.

"Hi, Lane. We just thought we'd drop in to see where you are in the investigation," Johnny said. He and Luke sat in the two chairs in front of the desk. Johnny hoped that subtly signaled to the lawman that they weren't going away without some answers.

Lane leaned back in his chair and released a deep sigh. "I wish I had something concrete to tell you. All we really know at this time is somebody was on the Black property and fired those two shots, and whoever it was, he was a damned good marksman. Both bullets slammed into your father's chest."

"Being a good marksman describes most every man in town," Luke said with obvious frustration in his voice.

"Almost everyone in town knew that my father was going to win the mayoral race. Have you talked to Wayne and Joe?" Johnny asked, referencing Wayne Bridges and Joe Daniels, the two men who had also been running for mayor against Big John. "Those two definitely had a motive to get rid of Dad."

"I've conducted an initial interview with them both, and now we're working to confirm their alibis," Lane replied.

"And what are their alibis?" Johnny asked. He knew both men had been highly competitive about the race, and just before the murder Wayne had begun nasty rumors and innuendos against Big John. However, the mudslinging hadn't stuck. Most everyone in town knew the truth about John's character, which was exemplary.

"Wayne was home with his wife, Martha, and she corroborated his alibi."

"Martha Bridges is as ambitious as they come. She'd lie in a heartbeat to protect Wayne," Johnny scoffed. "And what about Joe?"

"Joe claims he was out in his field at the time of the murder." Lane sat back up straight in his chair. "His ranch foreman confirmed that he was there."

"Who else have you spoken to? I know most of the people in this town liked my father, but I also know he made some enemies along the way," Johnny said.

"My men and I are in the process of working down the list of names you gave me right before the funeral."

"We know the shooter was on the Black property. Have you been able to locate specifically where the shooter stood?" Luke asked, his blue eyes darker than usual as he stared at Lane. It was an obvious sign that Luke was frustrated, as was Johnny.

"We have not. As you know that's a huge piece of property, and even knowing how far a rifle can shoot and the trajectory of the bullets doesn't narrow down the location much. We've walked the field in an effort to find anything left behind by the killer, but we found nothing, including shell casings." Lane shook his head. "I'm sorry, but at this point in the investigation, I don't have any more information for you. You know I'll keep you posted as the work continues."

Johnny released a deep sigh and stood, and Luke followed his lead by getting to his feet as well. "We need answers, Lane," Johnny said. "If you and your officers can't get them for us, then we'll work to get them for ourselves."

Lane got out of his chair, a deep frown cutting across his broad forehead. "Now, you know you need to leave the investigating to me. The last thing I need is for the two of you going off half-cocked and potentially ruining a case against the perpetrator. It's only been a week. We just need more time."

Johnny bit back a deep sigh of frustration. He knew he was probably being unreasonable in demanding answers after only seven days, but he wanted to know who had killed his father and why.

"Just keep us in the loop, Lane," he finally said.

"You know I will," the lawman returned.

"Well, that was a big waste of time," Luke said the moment they stepped out of the building.

"You've got that right," Johnny agreed. They both got back into the truck to head back home.

"As much as I want to know the who, I definitely want to know the why," Johnny said. "What would make somebody want to kill Dad?"

"My money is on Wayne. You know how badly he wants to win the mayoral seat, and Dad was in his way," Luke said.

"I just find it hard to believe anyone would commit murder over the mayoral position in a small town in Kansas," Johnny replied.

"Maybe he has bigger political aspirations, and becoming mayor is just the first step," Luke said.

"Maybe."

The two fell silent for several minutes. Luke cleared his voice. "Okay, I'm going to say something that's been on my mind and probably on yours as well…something that feels rather taboo."

Johnny shot his brother a curious glance. "Taboo? What are you talking about?"

"Caleb," Luke replied.

Johnny released the deep sigh that felt as if it had been trapped deep in his chest since his father's murder. "Surely you don't think Caleb shot Dad." There was no question that their younger brother had issues, but Johnny couldn't imagine him being a killer.

"I don't think Caleb would shoot Dad when he was sober, but who knows what condition he might have been in at the time? You know he drinks too much and God knows what kinds of drugs he takes. Nobody saw him until hours after the murder, and when Lane questioned him, he couldn't even say exactly where he had been when Dad was shot. And he and Dad had a huge fight the night before the murder." The words shot out of Luke with the force of an enormous internal pressure.

"A fight? I didn't know anything about a fight they had," Johnny said in surprise.

"Yeah, I didn't mention it to you before because I figured you had enough on your hands with executing Dad's will," Luke admitted.

"So, when exactly did this fight happen?"

"It was after dinner. You had already left to go back to your place, and I was just hanging around before going back to my house."

"Do you know what it was about?" Johnny's head reeled with this new information.

"Caleb wanted Dad to loan him money to open a storefront in town to sell his paintings, and Dad told him he needed to get out of the hayloft and off his artistic behind and do some work around the ranch before he'd even think about giving Caleb any money."

"How did Caleb react?" Johnny's hands tightened on the steering wheel as a new tension pressed hard inside his chest.

"He threw one of his usual temper tantrums. He said he hated Dad, who had never really loved him… yada yada," Luke said. "Caleb finally stormed out of the house."

"I should probably take this information to Lane," Johnny said reluctantly.

"Or not," Luke replied. "Maybe we keep this information under wraps for a bit and you and I investigate our brother. I don't want to throw Caleb under the bus without real evidence."

"That sounds good to me," Johnny instantly agreed. Besides, he found it almost impossible to believe that his youngest brother had killed his father in cold blood.

Johnny pulled up in front of his cabin, cut the engine and then turned in his seat to look at Luke. "What's on your agenda for today?"

"I thought I'd take Rod and Justin and head out to the south pasture to fix that fencing so we can get some cattle back in that area," Luke said.

Rod Jackson and Justin Albertson were two of the five ranch hands that lived in private rooms in the barn's hayloft. The rooms were as nice as some apartments, with each small unit having a bathroom complete with a shower.

"What's your plan for the rest of the afternoon?" Luke asked as the two got out of the truck.

"I think I'll take a quick ride on Lady, and then I've got a ton of paperwork waiting for me in the cabin."

"Anything I can help with?" Luke asked.

"No, it's still stuff I'm dealing with since Dad's death. Eventually I'll get to the end of it all." Johnny had been shocked by the amount of administrative tasks that had to be done upon a death, especially with all the business dealings his father had.

"Then I'll see you at dinner tonight." Luke waved and headed toward the barn. Since his father's death, all the siblings had been eating their evening meal together in the big house with their mother. Margaret was a strong woman, but she'd just been slowly recuperating from her bout with cancer, and being hit with Big John's death had nearly broken her.

Johnny headed for the stables, telling himself he needed a quick ride to clear his head, but deep down inside he knew there was another reason for it. It was just about this time of the day when he'd ridden out and found Chelsea reading in the old wagon. He wasn't sure why he wanted to see her again. He certainly didn't want to get involved with her in any way.

As he saddled up Lady, he thought about seeing

Chelsea at the funeral. There was no question that she'd looked sexy as hell in her short little black dress and with her dramatic hairstyle.

Despite the somber occasion, he'd instantly been filled with all kinds of unexpected memories of making love to her. There had been a time when he'd been positively addicted to her. Kissing her had always dizzied his senses, and the feel of her body pressed against his had been beyond wonderful. Hell, he'd even loved the very smell of her skin.

His addiction to her had gone far beyond the physical. The sound of her laughter had intoxicated him. A simple smile from her had once had the ability to create a well of happiness inside him. She had been the first thing on his mind when he'd awakened in the mornings and the last thing he'd thought about before going to sleep.

Of course, all those feelings had died five years ago when she'd turned her back on him and taken off for New York. He felt nothing for her now except a bit of curiosity about her time in the big city. At least, that's what he told himself, but as he approached the old wagon and saw her sitting there, curiosity didn't account for the sweet heat that suddenly rushed through him.

SHE HEARD HIM COMING, and she couldn't help the way her heartbeat quickened. Since the funeral, Chelsea had tried to put all thoughts of Johnny out of her head. She'd been shocked to realize that he was in a relationship with Tanya Brooks, a girl who had bullied Chelsea all through high school, and a woman who had been instrumental in Chelsea's decision to leave town.

Of course, none of that mattered now. Besides, she was certain that Johnny still hated her for what she'd done to him. Even though he'd been pleasant to her, that didn't mean there was a chance in hell for them to pick up where they had left off.

He'd moved on, as he should have, and no matter how many regrets she had for the choices she had made, it didn't change where they were in the here and now.

He came into view, looking as hot as ever on the back of his horse and with a black cowboy hat riding his head at a cocky angle.

Despite everything, she couldn't help the smile that curved her lips at the sight of him. She set aside the book she'd been reading as he pulled up in front of the wagon.

"Hi, Johnny," she said, pleased that her voice held none of the emotions that raced inside her. His black T-shirt stretched taut across his broad shoulders, and she knew he would smell like sunshine and the clean-scented cologne he'd always worn.

"Hey, Chelsea. Nice day to be outside."

"I love sitting out here to read. It's so peaceful and pleasant."

"It won't be too long before it will get too hot to sit outside," he replied.

"I'm hoping by then I'll be in my own place," she replied. "I've been looking, but there doesn't seem to be much available right now, at least not that I can find. What I'd really like is to rent or buy a house instead of living in an apartment."

"Do you have somebody helping you look? I know there are several empty houses in town, but I don't know who they belong to or if they would be an option for renting," he said. "If you want, I could check them out for you."

"Oh, I wouldn't want to impose," she protested.

"It's not an imposition if I offer," he returned with a smile.

"Then I would really appreciate it," she replied, trying to stanch the warmth that swept through her with his smile. Johnny had a beautiful smile.

He gave her a quick nod. "And I appreciated you showing up for the funeral."

"I wouldn't have missed it. Johnny, my heart just breaks for your family," Chelsea said with a wealth of emotion.

He looked off in the distance and then returned his gaze to her. "Thanks, Chelsea. I have to admit, it's been tough."

"I can't even imagine."

They fell silent for a few long moments. Once again it was a charged silence. "So, how long have you been dating Tanya?" she asked, then cursed herself. "I'm sorry. That's really none of my business."

He shrugged his broad shoulders. "It's no big secret. Tanya and I having been hanging out together for the last couple of months, although it isn't anything real serious right now."

His saddle creaked as he shifted his weight. "I know there was a time when Tanya wasn't very nice to you, but she's changed, Chelsea. She's kind and highly respected for her work with charities. She's a teacher, and the kids and parents really love her. I think you'll like her now."

When hell freezes over, Chelsea thought to herself. It was difficult to even think about forgiving the person who had made Chelsea's high-school years a complete nightmare. In any case, Chelsea couldn't imagine any reason for the two women to ever hang out together.

"That's nice to hear," she replied.

Again, an awkward silence descended. She stared off in the distance, where the old two-story house where she'd grown up was visible. That structure had never felt like home.

The Kings' house had been home, with Margaret always bustling in the kitchen and the sound of laughter ringing out and Johnny's blue eyes gazing at her with love.

Many evenings when she'd been growing up, she

could be found at the Kings' place enjoying the loving atmosphere that was lacking in her own home.

"Maybe you'd like to come over this evening to check out all the renovations I made to the foreman's cabin," he said.

She looked back at him in surprise. "I'd love to see the changes you've made."

"Then why don't you come by around seven this evening. Does that work for you?" he asked.

"Let me check my social calendar," she said jokingly. "Oh, looks like I'm free tonight." She smiled at him, and when he returned her smile, her heart warmed with myriad old emotions. His smile had always made her feel as if she was the only woman in the world, but she reminded herself that it was no longer hers to cherish.

"Then I'll see you this evening," he said. He reached up and readjusted his hat on his head and then turned his horse around and headed back toward the King home.

For the rest of the afternoon, Chelsea tried to tamp down her crazy emotions where the visit to Johnny's house was concerned. She shouldn't have taken him up on his invitation. There was no reason for her to see where he now lived. However, there was no question that she was curious about his life since she'd left him.

Was he curious about her life in the last five years? Or had he read the salacious tabloids and believed that she'd become a drug addict who had self-destructed, that she'd blown all her money on dope and had come home broke and scorned by the people who had once believed in her? Or maybe he believed that she had mental issues.

Or did he simply not care what had happened to her while she'd been gone? She was surprised he'd invited her to see the cabin and that he was being kind to her. She didn't deserve that after what she had done to him.

Perhaps he wasn't as affected by her leaving as she thought he'd been. Maybe soon after she'd left he'd realized he really wasn't in love with her and her breaking up with him had been a huge relief.

She shoved all these thoughts out of her head as she got ready for the evening. When she was finished dressing and applying her makeup, she looked at her reflection in the mirror.

The jeans fit tight on her long, thin legs, and the long-sleeved pink blouse hung below her hips and was slightly too large for her. She'd kept her makeup to a minimum…just mascara and lip gloss.

Bug-eyed skinny legs. That's what Tanya and her mean girlfriends had called Chelsea all through high school. *Alien creature*, they'd said with disdain. They'd had even worse names for her, and she'd never known exactly why she'd been chosen to be the girl scorned by them. She had a feeling it had to do with the fact that the handsome, popular Johnny King only had eyes for her.

As she went downstairs to leave the house, she wondered if Tanya would be at the cabin with Johnny. If so, then Chelsea would be nice and polite. She didn't have to like the woman to be civil.

"Where are you sneaking off to?" Stella sat on the overstuffed sofa in the living room with a magazine open in her lap.

Chelsea laughed. "If I was sneaking out, then I would have gone out my bedroom window and shimmied down the big oak tree like I did when I was a teenager."

"Where are you off to?" Stella asked testily.

"Johnny invited me over to see what he's done to the old foreman's cabin."

Stella put her magazine to the side and looked at Chelsea with interest. "Is it possible you two will get back together?" Stella didn't wait for Chelsea to answer but instead continued. "You were a fool to walk away from him in the first place. I'll never understand why you did that. It would be an honor for you to be a King."

"A reconciliation between us is out of the question," Chelsea said firmly. "So, get that thought right out of your mind."

"With Big John dead now, Johnny will be one of the most powerful people in the county. It would be a great move to merge our two families together."

"That has nothing to do with me. And in any case, he's dating Tanya Brooks."

Stella sneered. "That twit wouldn't stand a chance if you decided to go after Johnny."

"I'm not interested in going after Johnny. I'm not interested in dating anyone right now. We're just being friendly with each other. Now, I don't know when I'll be home, so don't wait up for me."

A moment later Chelsea stepped out the back door and into the cool, spring evening air. The only thing she carried with her was her cell phone, although she had nobody to call, and certainly nobody was calling her these days. Still, she figured she'd use the cell phone flashlight to help her get home after dark.

Not only did she want a place to live, but eventually she also needed to get herself a car. But even if she had one, she probably would have still walked to Johnny's cabin.

It had been years since she'd made the trek from her home to the old foreman's cabin, but her feet remembered the way without thought.

The cabin had been a favorite place for her to meet Johnny when they'd been young and wanted to be alone. At that time the structure had been sound, with a stone fireplace, a working bathroom and a living room and bedroom.

However, there had been no furniture, and several of the windows had been broken. There was no electricity, and mice had considered it a fine place to live. But she and Johnny hadn't cared about any shortcomings in the place.

Johnny had made a bed with hay beneath a thick blanket, and with a flashlight playing on the wall, they had spent hours there not only making love but also talking and planning their future together.

That was then…and this was now.

Twilight was falling, painting the landscape in shades of deep golds and purples. A half-moon spilled down a silvery light from the cloudless skies.

She'd always loved the smell of the pasture in the spring. It was the fragrance of sweet grass and a lingering hint of sunshine. It smelled of rich earth and wildflowers. It was the comforting scent of home.

She passed old outbuildings on her mother's property and then climbed a fence onto the King pasture. There were more outbuildings and thick-trunked trees and brush.

She hadn't gone too far when the hair on the nape of her neck rose, and she thought she heard footsteps behind her. She whirled around but saw nothing and nobody. Even though she didn't really need it, she flipped on her flashlight and shone it all around.

Nothing. She turned back around, turned off her flashlight and continued, laughing at her own jumpiness. And yet she couldn't shake the feeling that somebody was watching her as she hurried toward the cabin.

When it came into view, a small gasp escaped her. The place was at least three times larger than it had been before. The front of it looked homey with a covered porch that held two wicker rocking chairs and a planter colorful with pink and red flowers.

The closer she got, the more nervous she became, and she wasn't sure why. She and Johnny had known each other since they were kids, so what was there to be nervous about?

A rustling came from someplace behind her, and her nerves suddenly became about something much different than spending time with Johnny. She'd been a little bit on edge since coming home.

During her last year in New York, she had garnered the attention of a couple of rabid, scary fans. Even though it was highly unlikely that one of them had followed her here, an irrational fear filled her head.

More rustling sounded. She had no idea whether it was man or beast, but she wasn't going to turn around to find out. Fear torched through her. Her heart pounded loudly, deafening her to anything else, and her throat squeezed tight.

She raced as fast as she could the last few yards to the cabin and then knocked frantically on the door. When Johnny opened the door, she threw herself into his arms.

Chapter Three

"Whoa!" Johnny's arms automatically wound around Chelsea, and he held her trembling body tight against his own. "Chelsea…what's wrong? What's going on?"

She released a small laugh and quickly stepped out of his embrace. "Nothing is wrong… I—I'm so embarrassed. I just heard a lot of rustling noises on the way here, and I managed to freak myself out."

"There's a big old fox that wanders around this time of the night. That's probably what you heard." His body still retained the imprint of hers, even though he'd only held her for mere seconds. Her scent surrounded him, that lilac-and-vanilla fragrance that always stirred him.

He took a step back from her and opened his door wide enough to allow her entry. She stepped into the living room and instantly stopped, her gaze going around the room. "Oh, Johnny, this is beautiful."

A sense of pride filled him as he followed her gaze. Rich thick light gray carpeting covered what had once been rough plank flooring. The stone fireplace had been scrubbed clean to showcase the beauty of the natural rocks, and a thick wooden mantel held his flat-screen television.

An upholstered black sofa was flanked by smoked-glass end tables, and a matching coffee table stood before it. A black recliner completed the furnishings.

"I can't even believe this is the same place," she said.

"Come on, I'll give you the full tour," he replied. The kitchen had been updated with granite countertops and up-to-date appliances, and the small bedroom where they had once spent so many hours together had been transformed into a state-of-the-art office.

There were still times when he sat at his desk and thought he caught a whiff of her perfume lingering in the air. Before any of those memories could drag him back, he took her into the room he had built on.

It was a huge bedroom with a skylight in the ceiling. The king-size bed was covered with a navy spread, and there was nothing better than staring up at the stars as he drifted off to sleep. There was also a full bathroom, complete with a Jacuzzi tub and a shower.

"Johnny, it's absolutely breathtaking." She turned and looked at him. "You've transformed this place from a run-down old foreman's cabin into a beautiful home. You must be very proud of yourself."

"I am," he admitted and then gestured her toward the sofa in the living room. "Have a seat. Would you like something to drink? Some iced tea or a soda? Or perhaps a glass of wine?" He wasn't sure if offering her alcohol was even appropriate, given what he'd read in the tabloids about her.

"Actually, I'd love a glass of wine," she replied.

"Red or white? I have both." As she sank down on the sofa, he moved to the kitchen area. She looked beautiful tonight. The pink blouse enhanced her green eyes and blond hair and brought a light pink glow to her face. He could admire her without becoming emotional involved with her, he told himself firmly.

"White would be great," she replied.

He poured her glass of wine and took it to her and then went back and poured a glass for himself and grabbed a platter of sliced cheese and salami and crackers that he'd prepared minutes before she'd arrived.

He returned to the sofa and sat next to her, trying to ignore the evocative scent of her that drifted his way. "I made some phone calls this afternoon and found three houses that are empty here in town. Two are for sale, and one is for rent," he said.

"Thank you for finding out for me what's available. When can I see them?"

"If you want, I can take you to see all three of them tomorrow afternoon," he offered. Someplace in the back of his mind he wondered what in the hell he was doing.

Yet he also had a feeling why he was offering to spend some time with Chelsea. She was an easy distraction from the anger that gnawed at him over his father's murder, from the grief that clawed at his insides as he tried to keep his family together.

"Johnny, I'm sure you have much better things to do than escort me around town looking at houses," she protested.

"Chelsea, I'd be glad to take you to see them. Why don't I pick you up around one? Will that work for you?"

"Well, yes, but…"

"No *but*s," he replied.

She flashed him a smile that took him back to a place and time when she'd been his girl and all was right with the world. He cleared his throat and broke eye contact with her.

"Okay, thank you. But tell me about this place. It must have taken you a long time to get it like this," she said.

"It took me the better part of four years working on it nights and weekends to get it just the way I wanted it." There was no reason to tell her that it was the pain of losing her that had made him work so hard. He'd needed a project to focus on to keep his thoughts off her after she'd left him.

"Your hard work certainly shows. I especially

love the skylight in the bedroom." She smiled again. This time it appeared to be a bittersweet smile. "We always did like looking at the stars together."

Once again, he steeled himself for a new rush of emotions that fired through him. "I'll bet it was hard to see the stars at night in New York City."

She picked up a cracker and nibbled on it as she shook her head and then finally replied. "I lost sight of the stars while I was gone." She shook her head slightly again and then leaned back into the sofa cushion. "So, tell me what's happened while I've been gone. Are you still in touch with all the kids from high school?"

"Most of them. Sarah Crawley and Mick Kendall got married soon after you left town."

Chelsea laughed. "That girl chased him shamelessly all through high school. She was crazy in love with that guy. I even rode with her a couple of times past his house to see if she could just catch a glimpse of him before going to bed. I guess Mick got tired of being chased and finally let her catch him."

"They seem really happy together. They have a little boy, and she's pregnant again." He fought against a quick wave of wistfulness. He'd thought by this time he'd be married and have a couple of children.

"Good for them. Tell me more about who is with who and what's happened since I've been gone."

For the next two hours they ate crackers and

cheese and talked about what had happened in town over the last half decade. They laughed together as he related some of the more ridiculous things that had occurred in the small town…like when old man Leroy Simmons had gotten mad at his wife for not making his breakfast. Leroy had stormed into the café but had been in such a rage, he'd forgotten to put his pants on before leaving home.

He had always loved the sound of Chelsea's laughter. It was a tinkling, melodious sound that was not only pleasant on the ears but also contagious. He found himself searching for stories that he knew would make her laugh. They had always shared the same sense of humor.

Coyote Creek was a town that loved a party. There had been spring flings and Octoberfest celebrations that she had missed, and he tried to tell her the highlights of them all.

"I should probably head home," she finally said. It was just after nine. She stood, and he also got up from the sofa.

He walked with her to the front door, and she turned to face him. "It was nice visiting with you, Johnny. I've really enjoyed myself."

"I've enjoyed it too. I'll see you tomorrow at one so we can see about finding you a place to live."

As they moved closer to the door, she suddenly stood so close to him he could feel the heat from her body radiating out to his. He could smell the dizzying scent of her that had always stirred him.

All evening he had tried to ignore the slow burn of desire that she stoked inside him. But now he stood so close to her, and her lips were right in front of him, looking so achingly kissable.

Her eyes sparked brighter, and she leaned toward him just a bit. Oh, it was so damned tempting… But he stepped back and grabbed the doorknob, effectively breaking the moment. "Are you sure you're okay to get home?" he asked and opened the door. "I could always drive you back."

She smiled. "Johnny, I've made this journey from my house to yours and back a million times in the past. Now that I know there's a big old fox making all the rustling noises, I'll be just fine."

"Then I'll see you tomorrow at one," he said.

"Thanks, Johnny. Good night."

"Good night, Chelsea." He watched as she turned on the flashlight feature of her phone and then took off walking. He finally closed the door and walked over to the coffee table to clear the glasses and the remains of the cheese and crackers platter.

As he cleaned up, his mind whirled a million miles a minute, all with thoughts of Chelsea. He hated to admit to himself that she still had an enormous power over him.

It wasn't just the desire to make love to her again,

it was a desire to hold her when she was sad and to make her laugh whenever possible.

It was the desire to know all her secrets and to share his with her. She had not only been his lover in the past, she'd been his best friend.

Had she had somebody like that in New York? Had there been a man there who had stood beside her? Supported her through her troubles? Had there been a man in her life who had loved her as much as he had?

He'd seen a couple of publicity photos of her on the arm of some actor. Had he been her lover? Had he been the one who had loved and supported her? And had she loved him back?

He finished the cleanup and then sank back down on the sofa. He had to stay away from her. She was dangerous to his well-being and the peace of mind he'd finally found without her.

He had a feeling it would be so easy for him to fall in love with her all over again. He hadn't been enough for her before, and there was no reason to believe he would be now. Besides, he didn't believe that she was really here to stay permanently, no matter what she said.

He'd keep his word and show her the houses tomorrow, but after that he would go back to his life, and she could get on with building her life without him.

AS CHELSEA SLOWLY made her way toward her home in the distance, her thoughts were on Johnny. It had felt good to spend time with him again. She always felt safe and warm when she was in his presence. With him, she'd always felt like she was home.

A deep sadness swept over her as regrets once again weighed heavily on her heart. She wasn't sure why Johnny was being so nice to her, but she suspected she'd never have a chance to have more than a casual friendship with him.

She would never feel his lips on hers again or know the safety of his big strong arms around her. She would never again know the sweet slide of his naked body against her own.

And it was all her own fault. She could have been married to him, but she'd chosen another path. It had been a necessary move for her, and she didn't regret her personal journey, but she regretted that the cost of her own growth had been her relationship with Johnny.

She jumped as she heard a rustling noise behind her.

She turned around and used her light to look behind her. The light didn't do much to penetrate the darkness more than a few inches in front of her. Seeing nothing, a small, nervous laugh escaped her. That darned fox was going to give her a heart attack.

Once again, she forged forward, but the hair on the back of her neck rose as she again got the feeling of somehow being watched. She'd never been afraid of the dark before but, at the moment, she was more than a little bit creeped out.

More rustling filled the otherwise-silent night, and this time it was a loud noise that definitely sounded bigger than a fox running through the brush. She turned around and froze in horror.

Crashing through the brush and rushing toward her was a person dressed all in black. A ski mask covered the person's head, and he was swinging a scythe back and forth in a threatening manner.

The figure was like something out of a horror movie. Chelsea stumbled backward, terror cutting through her. Her brain sputtered, trying to make sense of what was happening. What…? Who…?

Her momentary inertia broke, and she turned and ran for home. Panicked sobs filled her throat, and her chest squeezed tight, making it impossible for her to scream.

Whish…whish…whish. The sound of the scythe slicing through the air just behind her absolutely petrified her. Oh, God, why was this happening? Who was this madman chasing her? She raced as fast as she could in an effort to stay ahead of the threatening person.

Her side ached, and her lungs burned. She threw a quick glance over her shoulder. The person was still coming. The scythe was still swinging. Oh, God, she had to run faster, faster! She couldn't let the person catch her.

She stumbled, slamming into the ground. Her phone crashed out of her hand, and the flashlight immediately shut off. Panicked and sobbing, completely out of breath, she still managed to quickly get to her feet and continue running as fast as she'd ever run in her life.

Whish…whish…whish. The scythe created the sound of death just behind her. Even as she ran, she couldn't believe this was happening to her. Who was the nightmare boogeyman who was chasing her…and why?

When she finally reached the back door of her house, she yanked it open, raced inside, locked the door and then slammed her back against it. She bent over, feeling nauseous as she tried to catch her breath.

She drew several deep, long breaths and then finally straightened up and moved the curtain aside on the door to peer outside. The moonlight shone down on the yard, and there was nobody there. No indication at all of the person who had chased her through the fields.

She leaned with her back against the door once again, frantically looking around the kitchen. What had just happened? Oh, God, what should she do? Fear still caused her to tremble uncontrollably.

Stella was one of those early-to-bed and early-to-rise kind of people. She would be sound asleep.

Besides, what could Stella do? Her gaze fell on the landline that Stella insisted they keep.

Call the police, a voice screamed in her head. She went over to the phone and picked up the receiver, but before she could dial, visions of the tabloid headlines screamed in her head.

Half the people in town probably thought she was a drug addict, and the other half probably believed she was mentally unstable. If she called Lane, would he really believe that a dark figure in a ski mask had chased her through the darkness wielding a scythe?

Or would he believe she had suffered some sort of a drug-induced hallucination? Would he believe she'd had a mental break with reality? She could just imagine the snickers and knowing glances that would follow her tomorrow if she called Lane. Heck, she could barely believe what had just happened.

A new sob escaped her, and she dropped her hand from the phone. *But it really happened*, a voice cried inside her. She wasn't mentally unstable, but a crazy person had chased her. And what would have happened if she'd been caught? Had the intent been to scare her half to death? Then it had succeeded. But what if the intent had been worse?

An icy chill trickled down her spine and pooled in the pit of her stomach. If things had been different, the first person she would have called would have been Johnny, but she didn't even have his phone number anymore. And in any case, she had no right to call him.

She remained in the center of the kitchen, a hand stuffed in her mouth to stanch the deep, retching sobs of terror that continued to work through her. She looked out the window once again, and still seeing nobody, she finally made her way upstairs to her bedroom.

Once there, she changed out of her clothes and into a nightshirt. She crawled into her bed and curled up into a fetal ball. Over and over, the visions of the scythe-swinging madman shot through her mind, making her shiver and cry.

She remained awake long into the night, her ears pricked for any sound that didn't belong. Would the person break into the house and hurt her? Had the person really gone away or was he waiting until the night deepened to make another move? Her heart continued to beat too quickly and fear iced through her. At some point she had fallen asleep and into nightmares that kept her tossing and turning.

Finally early-morning sun woke her. Even though she was still exhausted from the lack of any real sleep, she dragged herself out of bed and directly into a hot shower.

As she stood beneath the pelting spray, she found herself thinking about the hours she had spent with Johnny before the night had been hijacked by horror.

He'd transformed the old cabin into a beautiful

place to call home. If she hadn't made the choices she had years before, then that beautiful cabin would have been her home too.

There was no question that despite the years that had passed, in spite of all the experiences she'd had, she still had a wealth of love for Johnny in her heart.

He was the only lover she had ever known, and even now the idea of making love with anyone else was somehow repugnant. There had been many nights when she'd been alone in her East Side apartment in New York and she'd thought of him. There had been many times when she'd wanted to call him and share what was happening in her life, when she'd wanted to know what was happening in his.

Was he being nice to her now because he still had love for her in his heart? Was it possible they could reconcile after all this time and after what she'd done to him years before?

Maybe he was in love with Tanya now. Certainly, Tanya was a beautiful woman, and he'd spoken of her with great admiration. Chelsea would never step on Tanya's toes where Johnny was concerned, even though she owed Tanya no respect for the way she and her group of mean girl friends had treated Chelsea over the years.

No matter how she tried to distract herself with the pleasant evening she'd spent with Johnny, the horror of being chased intruded into her thoughts.

When she was dressed for the day she headed

downstairs, where her mother sat at the kitchen table with a cup of coffee and the morning newspaper before her.

"You're up early," Stella said without looking up from the paper.

"I didn't sleep very well, so when I saw the sun shining through the window I just decided to get up." Chelsea walked over to the counter, poured herself a cup of coffee and then sat at the table across from her mother.

"How did things go last night with Johnny?" Her mother picked up her coffee cup and peered at Chelsea over the rim.

"It was fine. He did an amazing amount of work on the cabin and turned it into a beautiful place." Chelsea wrapped her fingers around the warmth of her cup as she thought again about the night before. "It was scarcely recognizable from the little run-down cabin it had been."

"Did you tell him how stupid you had been to leave him?" Stella asked.

"We didn't talk about the past. We just visited for a little while."

"Any indication that he's still interested in you?"

"Mom, I told you before that Johnny and I aren't getting back together, so please leave it alone," Chelsea said.

Stella returned her attention back to the paper. For the next few minutes Chelsea drank her coffee and tried to get up her nerve to tell Stella what had happened to her on the way home from Johnny's place.

She drew a deep breath and released it slowly. "The reason I didn't sleep well last night is that something frightening happened when I was walking home last night."

Once again Stella gazed at her over the top of her cup. "Something frightening?"

"You're not going to believe this, but as I was walking home somebody dressed all in black and wearing a ski mask chased me with a scythe." The words exploded out of her on a single breath.

Stella slowly lowered her coffee cup to the table as she stared at Chelsea. Her upper lip curled and her gaze hardened. "I hope you didn't call Lane and bother him with such nonsense. Honestly, Chelsea, if you're taking some sort of drugs, then you need to stop it right now. If this is some sort of a wild ploy for attention, then you need to grow up. I'm running for mayor, and I won't have you bring me down with this kind of ridiculousness."

Her mother's words lashed at her, making her sorry she'd said anything at all. "Don't worry, I didn't call Lane. But it really happened. Somebody really chased me. I'm not on drugs, and I didn't just make it up."

Chelsea got up from the table and went out the back door. Once there she sank down on the stoop and fought against the tears that threatened to fall.

She should have known not to turn to her mother for support or comfort.

How she wished her brother was here right now! Jacob had always been a buffer between Stella and her. He would have believed Chelsea's tale, and he would be concerned about it…concerned about her.

She stared out toward the King place. She wasn't taking drugs. She had never taken any drugs. She hadn't made it up. Somebody had chased her last night with a scythe. Dammit, it had really happened.

She had no idea how long she sat there, feeling more alone than she'd ever felt in her life. She finally pulled herself up and put her self-pity away.

The first thing she wanted to do this morning was try to find her cell phone. Hopefully it hadn't been picked up by the person who had chased her or broken into pieces. She had a general idea where she had fallen and dropped it, so she now headed in that direction. She had no fear with the bright sun overhead.

She was glad she hadn't called Lane the night before. His response probably would have been just like her mother's, and the last thing she wanted was to be the topic of more gossip in the town.

Still, she couldn't help but wonder who had chased her and why. Who had wanted to terrorize her? Who had wanted to harm her? There was no question in her mind that if that person had caught her, she would have been badly hurt or killed. Thank God she had managed to run faster than her pursuer.

As she reached the part of the pasture where she thought she'd dropped her phone, she began running her feet through the thick grass, her concentration focused on the ground. The phone had a pink sparkly case, so it shouldn't be that difficult to see among the fresh, spring grass.

"What are you doing out here, Chelsea?"

She squeaked a surprise at Johnny's deep voice. She looked up to see him coming toward her. The sun shone on his dark hair and it was impossible not to notice the broadness of his shoulders beneath his white T-shirt. His worn jeans fit him to perfection.

Would her heart leap in her chest at any handsome man who looked so great, or was it just Johnny who made her heart quicken at his mere appearance?

"Chelsea?" He looked at her quizzically. "What are you doing?"

"I…uh…dropped my phone last night on the way back home from your place, and I'm looking for it." She averted her gaze from his.

"You dropped your phone? How did that happen?"

"Yeah…uh… I was running, and I tripped and fell, and it flew out of my hand."

She felt his gaze remain on her intently. "Why were you running?" he asked. "You know it's never a good idea to run through a pasture in the dark.

There are exposed roots and burrows and all kinds of things that can trip you up. Why were you running?"

"Uh… I don't know." The last thing she wanted was for Johnny to think she was crazy or on drugs too.

"Chelsea, look at me." He waited until she met his gaze again. "You know better than to run through a pasture in the dark, so why were you running? And why didn't you just pick up your phone after you dropped it?"

"I was running because I was being chased." She hadn't intended on telling him what had happened, but the words fell out of her. "I was being chased by somebody dressed all in black and wearing a ski mask and swinging a scythe. The person chased me, Johnny. I'm not on drugs, and I didn't make it up. It happened. It really happened."

The words exploded out of her fast and furiously, and hot tears filled her eyes. The terror that she'd felt the night before once again speared through her.

Then Johnny's big, strong arms were around her, holding her as she trembled and wept. God, she'd needed somebody to hold her. She'd desperately needed someone to tell her it was going to be okay and she was safe.

Even after her tears stopped, she remained in his embrace for several long moments. The scent of his fresh cologne soothed her. The feel of his body against hers quieted the fear that had momentarily been overwhelming.

She finally stepped away from him. "I'm sorry. I didn't mean to do that."

"Chelsea, I need you to tell me again what happened." A deep frown cut across his forehead.

She told him again, more slowly this time, about the person who had chased her. "I truly believe if he'd caught me, I would have been hurt or killed. Johnny, no matter what the tabloids speculated about me, they were wrong. I wasn't doing drugs while I was in New York. I didn't hallucinate this person, and despite my mother thinking I made all this up for attention, I didn't. It really happened, and it was terrifying."

"We need to call Lane," he said and pulled his cell phone from his pocket.

She placed her hand over his on the phone. "Are you sure you want to do that? He probably won't believe me."

Once again Johnny gazed at her intently. "Chelsea, I believe you, and Lane will believe me."

"I hope so," she replied fervently and dropped her hand back to her side.

She stared out over the field as Johnny made the call to Lane and asked him to come to his place. Nerves jangled in her veins.

Either Lane would believe her and Johnny, or

this would merely add to the notion that she was on drugs and either crazy or she was seeking attention.

Meanwhile, if the person had meant to kill her the night before, then he had been unsuccessful. How soon before he tried to do it again? Where would the next threat come from?

Chapter Four

As they waited for Lane to arrive, they both looked for her cell phone. Johnny's head reeled with what Chelsea had told him. Despite the fact that her story sounded outlandish, he believed her. Besides, he'd spent the whole evening with her and knew she hadn't been on any drugs and she'd only had one glass of wine. He also believed her when she said the tabloids had been wrong about her.

Chelsea had never been a liar, and despite what her mother thought, he'd never known Chelsea to be an attention-seeker. If she told him this had happened, then he believed her.

While he was highly concerned about what had happened to her, he wondered if it was really somebody trying to hurt him, or his family.

Had the person somehow mistaken Chelsea for Ashley? Was it possible the person had hoped to take out another King family member? Or had they known it was Chelsea and that in hurting her it would also hurt Johnny?

It was just an odd and very troubling thing to have happen right on the heels of his father's murder. Was it possible somebody was targeting his whole family?

These were definitely questions he intended to bounce off Lane when he arrived. They finally found Chelsea's cell phone. It appeared to be in good condition; however, the battery was dead.

They had just walked back to his cabin when Lane's car appeared. Within minutes, the three of them were seated in Johnny's living room and Chelsea was telling the police chief what had happened to her the night before.

"Could you tell if it was a man or a woman?" Lane asked when Chelsea was finished.

She frowned and slowly shook her head. "I have no idea. All I can tell you is he was definitely scary. I guess I just assumed it was a man considering how he swung the scythe. I'm sorry. I only got a brief glimpse of him because I was busy running."

"Did he say anything to you?" Lane asked.

Once again, she shook her head. "No. He didn't make a sound, which just made it all creepier."

Johnny sat next to her on the sofa and fought with his desire to put his arm around her and pull her close. At the moment her eyes were haunted with the revisit of the events of the night before and her body trembled slightly.

"Is there anything else you can tell me about the person?" Lane asked.

Chelsea released a deep sigh. "I'm sorry—no. Again, I was too busy running from him to notice much of anything. All I could hear was the sound of the scythe being swung just behind me, and I was afraid at any moment I'd be sliced with it."

"If you think of anything else, call me." Lane got up from the chair.

"I'll walk you out," Johnny said to Lane. "I'll be right back," he told Chelsea.

"Do you believe this story?" Lane asked the minute the two of them were outside.

"I do," Johnny replied firmly. "Remember, I've known Chelsea for years, and last night she wasn't impaired by any drugs. What I'd like to know is if the person was after Chelsea specifically or whether this was an attempt to hurt my family." He told Lane about the thoughts he'd entertained on the matter while looking for Chelsea's phone.

"I'd say at this point it doesn't matter what his motive was," Lane said as a deep frown cut across his forehead. "Is it possible he used your scythe? Because maybe I can pull some fingerprints off it."

"I don't even own a scythe," Johnny replied.

"I'll do my best to try to find the person, but without any more of a description, it's going to be difficult," Lane admitted. "I'll inform you if I learn anything."

Johnny didn't waste his breath asking about his father's case. He knew if Lane had any new information, he would have told him.

Once Lane was back in his car, Johnny returned to the cabin. "Tell me the truth, did he believe me?" Chelsea immediately asked.

"Of course he did," Johnny replied. "You should have called me last night and told me what had happened."

"I don't have your phone number," she replied.

He looked at her in surprise. "It's the same number it's always been."

"Oh, I just assumed you'd changed it…uh… before, I mean after…" Her voice trailed off.

He had never considered changing his number after she'd left Coyote Creek. There had been a part of him that had hoped she would call him, that she would miss talking to him. But she'd never called. "Do you still have it?"

She nodded affirmatively and then stood. "I need to get out of your hair now."

"Chelsea, if anything like this happens to you again, I want you to call me immediately," he said. "I'll drive you home," he added, not wanting her to take the walk through the pasture alone again.

"That's really not necessary. I'm not afraid as long as the sun is shining."

"But there's no reason for you to walk back if I can drive you," he countered. She might not be afraid in the sunlight, but he knew very well evil could come in the daytime. His father had been shot on a beautiful, cloudless day.

Minutes later they were in his truck, and he was headed to the Black house. "Are we still on for this afternoon?" he asked.

"As far as I'm concerned we are, but it's up to you. I've already taken up most of your morning. Maybe you need the afternoon to catch up."

"No. Besides, I know how eager you are to find a place, so we're still on for one o'clock." He pulled up in front of the two-story house.

"Thanks, Johnny. I'll be ready."

He watched as she walked up to her front door, and once again countless questions flew through his head. Who had donned a ski mask and chased her through the pasture swinging a scythe? And why? Who had murdered his father, and why?

The questions continued to plague him until he pulled back up in front of the Black house. Chelsea flew out the door, a vision in white capris and a yellow blouse. Between the blouse and her bright smile, she looked like a ray of sunshine.

"I'm so excited," she said as she got into the passenger seat. "I can't wait to view these places and see if one of them will be my future home."

"The first one I'm taking you to is the rental. It's the nicest of the three," he said.

As they headed into town, they engaged in small

talk. One of the things he had always admired about Chelsea was her ability to compartmentalize. When her mother yelled and said horrible things about her, she would tell Johnny about it and then was able to quickly move past it.

Now, it was obvious she'd put the night's horror behind her and was totally invested in the potential of finding a place to live.

He pulled up in front of the attractive ranch house for rent. "Oh, it's nice," she said. The house was painted a light brown with darker brown shutters. A flowerbed was full of petunias, and the lawn was perfectly manicured.

A few moments later Johnny put in the combination that would open the lockbox and provide a key. They stepped into a nice-sized living room with what appeared to be new beige carpeting and freshly painted walls.

"It's a very nice place," she said after they'd walked through. "But I was really hoping to buy a house, and in any case this one just doesn't speak to me."

He'd been sure she'd choose to move in here where the house was in perfect move-in condition and the monthly rent was on the low side.

"Okay. Then let's go see the next one," he replied.

The next house was a two-story. There was a wraparound porch with an unsteady railing that needed repairs, and the house could use a coat of paint.

"This one is owned by the bank," he said as he unlocked the door. "It's been empty for about a year."

They walked into a large living room with a fireplace on one wall. The walls also needed fresh paint. He followed her as she went into the kitchen and then climbed the stairs to the second floor.

He remained at the top of the stairs as she checked out the three bedrooms and the bathroom. She came out of the master bedroom and practically danced down the hall toward him.

"Oh, Johnny, I love this house. There's even a big tree outside the master-bedroom window that reminds me of the one outside my bedroom in Mom's house."

Her eyes sparkled with excitement, and when she reached him she wrapped her arms around his neck and kissed him on the cheek.

He froze, the familiar feel of her in his arms shooting a swift, unexpected desire through him. Thankfully she stepped back from him before he could do something stupid like capture her lips with his.

"There's no need to show me the last house. This is the one I want. I love everything about this one. I can totally see myself here," she said.

They headed back downstairs and went outside to his truck. "Are you sure this is what you want?" he said before starting his engine. "This place is going to require some work."

"That's okay. It's mostly just cosmetic stuff. Surely there's a handyman here in town I can hire to take care of things."

Johnny started the truck. "Jeb Taylor is a reputable handyman. I'll give you his phone number, and I also need to give you the phone number of my contact at the bank who can help you with the house."

"Oh, I'm so excited. I can't wait to be in that house and out of my mother's place," she said. "Although, I have to be honest, staying with Stella has been so stressful I was ready to find an empty rabbit burrow and move in there."

He smiled. "Thank goodness it didn't come to that. I'm just glad you found something you like." He could still feel the heated imprint of her lips against his cheek. She was still in his blood, but now that he had fulfilled his promise to take her to see potential places for her to live, he intended to walk away from her.

It was time he got back to his own life...a life without Chelsea in it. It was also time for her to build whatever life she wanted.

Despite the fact that she intended to buy the house, he still wasn't convinced she'd stick around. Coyote Creek would be a pretty boring place after the excitement and bright lights of New York City. How long before she longed for the city that never slept?

In any case, she'd broken his heart once, and

there was no way he was giving her a chance to do it again.

When they reached Stella's place, he gave her the phone numbers she needed, and they said their goodbyes. As he drove home she remained in his thoughts.

He had a feeling there was a part of him that would always love Chelsea. She'd been his first lover, and for a long time he'd believed she would be his wife and the mother of his children.

There was no question that her return to town had shaken him up, stirring old memories of passion and love. He'd finally gotten to a place where he'd moved past her, but seeing her and spending time with her again had thrown him off his game. But it was time he shoved memories of Chelsea away.

Once he went back to the ranch, he busied himself with the chores he had missed that morning, and then it was time to go inside for dinner with his family.

As the King family all came together for the evening meal, the head-of-table chair remained empty. It was an emptiness that screamed inside Johnny. It was a cry of pain, of anger and grief, over his father's absence.

Dinner was provided by a woman Big John had hired when his wife had first gotten ill. Nellie Maddox was in her midsixties and lived in one of the spare rooms in the house. She was a great cook and provided all three meals for the King family.

Tonight, she had made a feast of fried chicken, baked beans and coleslaw. There was also a Jell-O salad and golden corn bread with honey butter.

As they ate, Johnny tried to engage each of them in conversation. Luke appeared to be deep in his own head, not eager for any small talk directed at him.

Ashley was also unusually quiet, answering questions in one or two words. Caleb appeared to be in his own head too. But that wasn't unusual for him. Finally, there was their mother. Margaret looked drawn and tired and still appeared achingly fragile.

When the meal was over, Johnny walked to his cabin, his thoughts troubled. Somebody had murdered his father, and law enforcement didn't have a clue as to the criminal. Somebody had chased Chelsea across the pasture wielding a scythe. And he felt like his family was falling apart.

He knew his father would expect him to keep the family going, but right now they didn't feel like a family at all. They all appeared to be on separate islands with no way to bring them all together.

Right now his father would be disappointed in him for not being able to accomplish that. Big John had always stressed the importance of the family.

God, he missed his dad. Every day when doing the chores, he longed for his dad's voice, longed to hear his deep, raucous laughter. He missed the conversations they'd shared, talks where his dad had always imparted some nugget of wisdom to him.

For the most part Johnny had few male friends. It had always been enough to have his father and Luke as his best friends. But his dad was now gone, and Luke had become distant, and Johnny realized he was lonely for the male bonds he'd had with both of them.

His dark and troubling thoughts continued to plague him throughout the evening. When darkness came and bedtime rolled around, he realized he was too restless to settle in.

Instead of getting into bed and waiting for sleep to come, he stepped outside with the idea of walking around, in the hopes of tiring himself out.

The night was dark, but the moon reflected light with no clouds to hinder it. Night insects clicked and whirred with their songs as he headed up the path that would take him to the barn.

He walked slowly, trying to tell himself that he needed to let go of the things he couldn't control. He had no control over the investigation Lane was conducting into his father's death and now Chelsea's attacker.

He also had little control over how his family members were dealing with Big John's death. He could only hope with more time and with his continued steadying support, they would all come back together again, stronger than ever.

He reached the side of the barn and leaned with his back against the wood. He stared up at the stars overhead and wondered what Chelsea was doing tonight.

Had she called the bank and made the arrangements to buy the house? Could she even get a mortgage without having a job? He frowned. It was none of his business and not his problem, he reminded himself.

He needed to call Tanya and set up a date with her for the coming weekend. Even though he wasn't in love with her, he did enjoy seeing her and spending time with her occasionally. He felt no pressure from her to deepen their relationship, which was good.

He had a feeling he would never love another woman like he had loved Chelsea. She had imprinted so deep in his heart there wasn't room for another woman...at least, not yet.

Maybe someday there would be room for somebody else. He wanted that. He wanted a woman who would be his best friend, who would always have his back and would love him deeply.

He wanted a woman he could love deeply, one who he would protect with his life and would give him the family he longed to have. So far, the only woman who had ever filled all his wants and needs had been Chelsea. There had to be another woman out there for him. He'd just have to be patient until she came along.

With a deep sigh he started to head back to his cabin, but something caught his eye…movement in the pasture. He narrowed his eyes and realized it was a man walking across the landscape.

Who in the hell would be in his pasture at this time of night? Visions of somebody chasing Chelsea filled his head. Was it the same person? Why would anyone be out here?

Adrenaline flooded through his veins. He took off, half-running after the person. He ran as quietly as possible, but when he drew closer the person must have heard him approaching. The trespasser threw a glance over his shoulder, and then he started to run.

Johnny hadn't gotten a good enough look to be able to identify the interloper, but he raced as fast as he could in an effort to catch him.

"Hey…stop," Johnny yelled. Not only was it suspicious for a person to be out here but it was even more suspicious that he was running in an effort not to be caught.

Dammit, normally Johnny would wear a gun when he was outside, but he'd been so distracted tonight he'd neglected to grab it before leaving his cabin. While he would never shoot a man in the back, he would have fired a warning shot that might have stopped the man in his tracks.

Unfortunately, he didn't have his gun. He ran as

fast as he could, his breaths coming in labored gasps as he was determined to catch the person.

He began to gain on the man, and he pushed himself even harder. Knowing it was possible this was the same perp that had tormented and threatened Chelsea, he was damned and determined that the creep wasn't going to get away.

He finally got close enough to lunge at the person. He hit him in the shoulders, and they both went down to the ground. "Okay…okay," the man said and allowed Johnny to pull him to his feet.

It was then Johnny recognized him. "Leroy Hicks…what in the hell are you doing out here on my property?"

Leroy was a small man with pinched features and a long nose that gave him a face that resembled a weasel. Six months ago he'd worked as a foreman for Big John, but he had been fired for misappropriation of funds and for being drunk on the job on numerous occasions.

Two things quickly flew through Johnny's head. The first was that right at this moment Leroy reeked of alcohol. The second was that he hadn't thought about Leroy when he'd given his list of potential suspects to Lane.

"I was visiting with Caleb," Leroy replied defensively. "Last I heard, visiting a friend wasn't against the law."

"Why didn't you leave by the main entrance? What are you doing trekking across the pasture?"

Leroy shrugged. "Stella hired me a week ago, so I've been living in her foreman's cabin, and the easiest way to get from Caleb's place to mine is through the pasture."

Why on earth would Caleb be interested in getting together with a lowlife like Leroy, a man their father had fired and who had wished all kinds of bad things on Big John and his ranch?

"Why don't we go have a little chat with Caleb," Johnny said, unsure he believed the man about visiting with his youngest brother.

Leroy shrugged again. "Fine with me."

The two men began the walk back to the Kings' barn. They walked in silence, but Johnny's head was filled with suppositions and possibilities.

Was Leroy the person who had chased Chelsea? Certainly Leroy knew that harming her would ultimately hurt Johnny. When Big John had fired the man, Leroy had vowed vengeance on the King family.

Johnny couldn't believe he'd forgotten all about Leroy when he'd made his list of potential suspects for Lane. First thing tomorrow morning he'd call Lane to add the former foreman to the list.

They finally reached the barn. Bales of hay rose up on one side of the large structure. There were four rooms on the second floor that were occupied by four of the men who worked for the ranch. Caleb's room was on the first floor.

Johnny strode to the door and knocked rapidly. There was no answer. He knocked once again. "Okay, okay, I'm coming," Caleb's voice rang out.

A moment later Caleb opened his door. The smell of pot and booze drifted through the doorway. Caleb stared at Johnny and Leroy. "What's going on?"

"I caught Leroy out in our pasture, and he said he'd been visiting you," Johnny said.

"He was." Caleb narrowed his eyes. "Is that a problem? Are you trying to tell me who I can or can't be friends with, Johnny? That's something Dad always tried to do. But now Dad is dead, and I don't have to listen to him anymore. He doesn't get to ride my back anymore. I definitely don't have to listen to you about anything, including who my friends are."

Johnny nearly stumbled backward beneath his brother's venomous tone. He drew in a deep breath and released it. "You are a grown man, Caleb. You can certainly pick your own friends. I just wanted to confirm that Leroy had been here with you."

"Yeah, he was here. We've become good friends," Caleb replied with a lift of his chin. "He likes my artwork and believes I have a lot of talent. So, are you done with me now?" Before Johnny could reply Caleb slammed his door shut.

Johnny turned to Leroy. "I'm sorry I bothered you, but I suggest in the future you come and go from the main entrance of the ranch. Skulking around in the dark in the pasture isn't a good idea. It could get you shot."

"Got it," Leroy replied. Together the two men left the barn, and Johnny watched as Leroy headed down the path that would lead him to the driveway.

Johnny frowned as he watched Leroy go. Was it possible he was the man who had chased Chelsea the night before? Yes, it was possible.

He was definitely shocked that his brother was friendly with Leroy. Equally as shocking was Caleb's brief diatribe. As Johnny walked back to his cabin, his head felt like it was going to explode with all the disturbing thoughts whirling around.

Along with the things that were already bothering him he now had a bigger, darker thought in his head. He hadn't really considered it a viable option when Luke had brought it up, but it now felt far more possible.

On top of all the other troubling thoughts that weighed heavily on his mind, he now had a deeper, darker question adding to his burden.

Had Caleb killed his father? Was Johnny's brother a cold-blooded killer? The possibility seemed much stronger now and shot a new cold dread into the pit of Johnny's stomach.

Chapter Five

It had been ten days since Johnny had shown Chelsea this house, and the past ten days had been a flurry of activity. She had bought the house, a surprisingly easy process due to the fact that she'd paid cash for it and hadn't needed to apply for a mortgage.

She'd immediately hired Jeb Taylor, an affable man in his midfifties who had a shiny bald head and beautiful green eyes. He'd gone to work on painting all the rooms on the lower level. He worked hard and fast. He wasn't much of a talker, but he did great work.

When the painting on the lower level was finished, Chelsea had bought new furniture for the entire house, and tonight she was welcoming her very first houseguest.

She now checked on the cheese enchiladas to make sure they were cooking nicely. She stirred the rice and then began to pour tortilla chips into a bowl.

Except for the brief sighting at John's funeral, she hadn't really seen Melinda since the two had left New York and returned to Coyote Creek. However, she had heard through the grapevine that Melinda was back with the boyfriend she'd dated before she'd left town.

Chelsea hoped her friend was happy. Melinda had supported the two of them when they'd first arrived in the big city. She'd gone to work at a deli a block away from the tiny West Side apartment they'd rented. While Chelsea had been hitting the sidewalks looking for a modeling agency who would take her on, Melinda had worked fifty- and sixty-hour weeks to pay the bills.

When Chelsea hit it big, she had rented a nice apartment on the East Side for herself and one for Melinda. She'd put Melinda on her payroll, and she no longer needed to work in the deli.

Chelsea shook her head with a smile. She and Melinda had eaten mac and cheese for months before Chelsea had begun to make money.

At least tonight there was no mac and cheese on the menu. Chelsea had chosen a cheerful yellow dish set, and with the chips and salsa in bright red bowls the table looked quite festive.

She checked her watch and scurried up the stairs to get dressed and put on a little makeup before Melinda arrived. Her bedroom was only half-painted, and since it was Saturday, Jeb wouldn't be back until Monday to continue the work.

She removed the housedress she'd worn all day

and changed into a pair of jeans and a navy blue blouse. After lightly applying cosmetics, she went back down the stairs.

Once in the living room she plumped the pink and yellow throw pillows on the white sofa. The end tables held lamps that most people would describe as *blingy*, and the coffee table held a beautiful candle arrangement.

The space had started to truly feel like home. The only thing missing was somebody for her to share it with. A vision of Johnny filled her head.

She'd heard and seen nothing of him in the past ten days, although he'd never been far from her thoughts. Every time he popped into her mind, she consciously tried to shove him out. It was obvious he had no intention of pursuing any kind of a relationship with her, nor did she really expect him to.

There would always be a sadness in her heart where he was concerned. She would always regret leaving him all those years ago, even though it had been necessary at the time. Now she just had to live with her choice. He was living the life he'd been leading before she'd returned to town, and she had to figure out what her life was going to be like moving forward.

Before she could get too much deeper into her thoughts, her doorbell rang. She reached the front door and pulled it open, then smiled at the dark-haired, slightly plump woman who had been her best friend for years.

"Melinda, come on in." Chelsea opened the door wider to allow Melinda entry, and the two hugged.

"Oh my goodness, Chels, I can't believe how nice you've made it in here," Melinda exclaimed as she looked around the living room. "Everything smells so new."

Chelsea laughed. "That's because everything is new."

"I would have known this was your place just by peeking in the window," Melinda said.

"How?" Chelsea asked.

Melinda laughed. "Who else in Coyote Creek would have pink throw pillows on their sofa?"

Chelsea grinned at her friend. "Come on into the kitchen. I've got dinner ready and your favorite brand of tequila waiting for you."

Melinda followed Chelsea where she motioned her guest to the kitchen table. "Sit and enjoy the chips and salsa, and I'll pour you a tequila shot."

"Sounds good to me." For the next few minutes, the two women drank their shots, ate chips and caught up with each other.

"I heard you and Roger were back together," Chelsea said. Melinda and Roger Simmons had been a couple before Melinda had left Coyote Creek with Chelsea.

"Yeah, I couldn't believe it when he showed up

at my parents' house to see me. I figured he'd probably got married while I was gone, but he told me he'd just been waiting and hoping that I'd wind up back here. It all just seemed easy and natural. It was as if the last five years didn't happen."

"That's so sweet. I always said that Roger is the nicest man in Coyote Creek," Chelsea said.

"He is a real sweetheart," Melinda agreed.

"Are you ready to settle down with him?" While in New York and once Melinda had become Chelsea's secretary and publicity person, she had become quite the party girl. While Chelsea stayed home night after night all alone, Melinda was out at bars and parties almost every night. Chelsea's name had gotten Melinda into a lot of posh parties.

She now smiled at Chelsea. "I think all my wild days are finally behind me, so yes, I'm ready to settle down with Roger."

"Then I'm happy for you." Chelsea stood. "Now, I've got some cheese enchiladas and Mexican rice that I made just for you."

"Ah, you know how much I love your enchiladas."

Chelsea pulled the meal out of the oven and set the dish in the middle of the table. She then put the rice in a serving bowl and added it to the table.

"So, what's going on with you and Johnny?" Melinda asked as they filled their plates.

"Absolutely nothing is going on with us. He was

very kind and helped me find this place, but I haven't seen or heard from him since."

"I was wondering, because Roger and I saw him out Saturday night at the café with Tanya Brooks. Roger told me they'd been dating for a while."

"Yeah, I knew he was seeing her," Chelsea replied and tried to ignore the swift pang in her heart.

"That's got to really chap your hide," Melissa said. "She and her friends were so crappy and hateful to you for so many years."

"Johnny told me she's changed, that she's really nice and kind and well-respected now."

Melinda snorted. "That's a load of cow manure. A leopard doesn't change its spots, and you'll never convince me that Tanya has changed her personality. She's always had a big core of hatefulness inside her, and she and her friends were positively cruel to you."

Chelsea shrugged. "I guess she's Johnny's problem now." A tiny spear once again shot through her heart. Of all the people Johnny could be dating, why did it have to be a woman who had been so mean to her?

"I heard some news about your mother this morning. She's running for mayor?"

Chelsea released a deep sigh. "Yes, she is."

"How is good old Stella doing?"

"You know Stella. As long as it's all about her she's happy. She decided to run for mayor after Big John King's murder."

Melinda's brown eyes widened. "What's up with that? Does Lane have any clue as to who is responsible?"

"Last I heard he had no clue." Chelsea hesitated a moment and then told Melinda about the wild chase through the pasture from Johnny's place.

"Oh, my God, girl! That must have been absolutely terrifying." Melinda reached across the table, grabbed Chelsea's hand and squeezed it tightly. "Thank God you managed to get away."

"It was more than terrifying." A cold shiver threatened to walk up Chelsea's spine at the memory. "I truly thought I was going to die."

"Why didn't you call me and tell me about this right after it happened?"

"Oh, Melinda. Everything seemed to go by in a whirlwind. Johnny had me call Lane to investigate the incident, and then I bought this place and there was so much work to do."

"That's okay, I forgive you, and I'm here now." Melinda served herself another enchilada. "Do you miss New York at all?"

"Not one bit," Chelsea replied truthfully. "You know I was ready to come home long before I was cast out."

"I just didn't understand it. You were riding so high. You had the whole world at your feet."

"Not without paying a heavy price," Chelsea countered. "It was definitely a wild ride," she added.

Melinda laughed. "It was that. Remember those nights when we thought it was a real treat to add a little hamburger to our mac and cheese?"

Chelsea laughed. "I was just remembering those mac-and-cheese nights earlier."

They finished eating and then moved into the living room for more girl talk. Melinda had been out in town more than Chelsea, so she had heard all the latest gossip, which she happily shared with Chelsea.

The two laughed as they reminisced about both their time in the big city and their years in high school. Chelsea had spent many sleepovers at Melinda's house where the two had plotted revenge on Tanya and her friends. They had been ridiculous, over-the-top revenge plots that had never been acted on, but at the time it had been fun to talk about.

At eleven o'clock Melinda called it a night. "We have to get together again soon. Maybe one night later in the week we can go to the Red Barn and drink a little and kick up our heels," she said as Chelsea walked her to the front door. "Roger can be our designated driver, and it would be good for you to get out socially."

The Red Barn was a popular bar and dance hall on the outskirts of town. "That sounds like a plan. I know I need to get out a little more often. I haven't even had a meal in the café yet."

"You definitely need to get out and see who is

on the market. We've got to find you a nice, sexy boyfriend."

Chelsea laughed. "Maybe before I get a new boyfriend I need to figure out what I want to do as far as a job is concerned."

"Ah, you can't fool me. I know you banked all the money you made as a top model. With the low cost of living here, you probably will never have to work again," Melinda replied.

"I need a job for my own peace of mind. I need to feel productive. It really has nothing to do with money," Chelsea replied. She opened the door where outside the night's darkness was broken up by a nearby streetlight.

"Call me, and we'll set up a night later this week or next week to go out," Melinda said as the two hugged.

Minutes later Chelsea closed and locked her front door and then returned to the kitchen to clean up the dinner dishes and take care of the leftovers.

As she worked, a smile curved her lips. She always felt good after spending time with Melinda. Melinda was bright and funny and had always had Chelsea's back. She had a wicked sense of humor and had always been able to make Chelsea laugh.

Although going out to the Red Barn wasn't really Chelsea's thing, she knew it would be far too easy for her to become a hermit here in her home.

She'd thought about approaching Ashley about a

job in her shop. When Chelsea had been at the grocery store the day before, she'd seen that the store had reopened.

The idea of working there was more appealing than sacking groceries or working as a waitress. However, she didn't want to ride on the fact that she'd once been Ashley's brother's fiancée.

The last thing she wanted was for Ashley to somehow feel obligated to give Chelsea a job. Chelsea believed she'd know if Ashley might hire her out of some kind of pity, and that was the last thing Chelsea wanted.

She finished clearing the dishes, and with the leftovers safely stored in the fridge, she finally made her way upstairs. The master bedroom was half-painted a creamy beige, and she had chosen contemporary furniture that included a makeup vanity. At the moment the furniture was all shoved toward the center of the room to aid Jeb's painting.

She now sat at the vanity to take off her makeup. Once it was removed, she stared at her reflection. She had made the mistake of taking on and believing Tanya's words…that she was ugly and strange-looking.

Johnny had always made her feel beautiful, but deep down she hadn't really believed him. It had taken five years for Chelsea to finally embrace her appearance, to reach an inner peace she'd desperately needed. It had been her personal journey and one she'd needed to leave Johnny and Coyote Creek behind to attain.

She got up from the vanity and opened a drawer to retrieve her nightshirt. Stifling a yawn, she changed into the thigh-high cotton garment and then got into bed.

She'd been so busy over the last week and a half she now felt completely exhausted. She curled up beneath her sheets and almost immediately fell asleep.

She jolted wide awake and shot upright, her heart racing a million beats a minute. What? What was going on? What had suddenly awakened her in a flight-or-fight state of mind?

Had it been a bad dream that had jerked her awake? If so, she didn't remember anything about it. Then she heard it. A tinkling of something coming from downstairs.

What was that noise? She hadn't really been in the house long enough to be familiar with all the sounds it might make in the night. Was it some strange water trickle through the pipes? Did a neighbor have a wind chime hanging in a tree that was clinking in a breeze?

The noise halted for a moment and then resumed. Chelsea slid out of bed and grabbed her cell phone off the nightstand. She turned on the flashlight feature and slowly walked down the stairs, her heart still pounding fast and furiously.

She was halfway down the stairs when she realized the noise was the sound of breaking glass. She turned off the flashlight as the moon drifting into the windows made enough light for her to see.

The noise seemed to be coming from the kitchen, and she headed there. The minute she entered the room she saw him…the same dark figure wearing a ski mask and breaking the panels of glass near the doorknob in her back door.

She screamed, and the figure looked up. Pure hated glared from the person's eyes. She screamed again and then remembered she had her cell phone in her hand. She quickly punched in the emergency number, but when she looked up again the figure was gone.

As she told the dispatcher her name and address, she grabbed the biggest, sharpest knife from the butcher block on the countertop and held it tightly in her trembling hand.

Where had he gone? Had he moved to another window someplace else in the house? Where? She tried to listen to see if she could hear breaking glass anywhere else, but all she could hear was the frantic beat of her heart pounding in her head and the panicked gasps of terror that escaped her.

What if he managed to break in before help arrived? The kitchen clock read 2:00. Nothing good happened at this time of the morning. If she hadn't heard that first tinkle of glass and awakened, what would have happened to her?

Would he have entered the house and silently crept up the stairs to her bedroom? Would he have raped her? Killed her? Oh, God, what was taking so long for the police to get here?

She clutched the knife tightly and prayed she wouldn't have to use it, but she would definitely do so to save her own life. In the other hand she still held her phone. Johnny. He had told her to call him if anything like this happened again.

She hesitated a moment and then punched in his number. He answered on the second ring, his voice husky with sleep. "Johnny," she said and then burst into tears.

"CHELSEA, WHAT'S GOING ON?" Johnny clutched his cell phone to his ear and at the same time he sat up and turned on the lamp on his nightstand.

"That man…that man is here. He tried to b-break in." The words came amid sobs. "He…he was at my back d-door and breaking the gl-glass to get in."

"Hang up and call Lane," he instructed as he got out of bed.

"I…already called, but n-nobody is here yet."

Johnny could hear the abject terror in her voice, and an icy fear shot through him. "Where are you now?"

"I'm in the kitchen."

"Get to the bathroom and lock yourself in. Do you hear me? Lock yourself in the bathroom, and I'll be there as quickly as I can," he instructed.

"Please hurry. I don't know where he is now, and I'm so scared."

"Just get to the bathroom. Lock the door, and don't open it for anyone but me or the police." He hung up and quickly dressed. He then strapped on his gun and left his cabin. Any residual sleepiness he might have felt was instantly gone, replaced by a sharp edge of tension that tightened his chest.

It took him only moments to get into his truck and head into town. As he drove his mind worked overtime. First and foremost, he prayed that she had done what he told her to and was now locked behind another door.

If this was the same person who had chased her through the pasture, then it had nothing to do with his family and everything to do with Chelsea.

Who was after her and why? As far as he knew, she hadn't had any issues with anyone. The way he'd heard it, she'd scarcely been out of her house since buying it. So, the same questions repeated in his head…who was after her and why?

He drove as fast as he possibly could without getting reckless. The terror in her voice had frightened him. What was happening now? Had the man managed to get inside the house? Was she being attacked right this very minute? Or had the police finally shown up?

She was all alone with a madman attempting to break into her house. Again he hoped she had done what he'd told her and locked herself in the bathroom. At least that would be one more barrier for the intruder to get through if he did get into the house.

When he turned the corner of her street, he breathed a deep sigh of relief as he saw two patrol cars, with their red and blue lights swirling, parked in her driveway. Hopefully they had gotten there in time to catch the culprit and save Chelsea from any harm.

He parked against the curb and then jumped out of his truck and raced toward the house. The front door was open, and when he walked in, he saw Chelsea seated on the sofa looking small and vulnerable in a hot-pink nightshirt. Lane and two other officers were standing by.

The minute Chelsea saw him she flew off the sofa and into his arms, sobs racking her body. "Shhh," he soothed her as he patted her back. "It's okay... You're safe now." As she continued to cry, he shot a helpless look at Lane, who shrugged back at him.

She cried for several long moments and then finally pulled herself together, although her body still trembled as he continued to hold her.

Finally, she stepped out of his arms and returned to her seat on the sofa. "Somebody tried to break in through her back door," Lane said before Johnny could ask.

"It was the same person who chased me through

the pasture," Chelsea said. "He hates me. Whoever it is hates me and wants me dead."

"Have you had any problems with anyone here in town?" Lane asked her.

"No…nobody. I've kept a pretty low profile since I've been back here," she replied in a trembly voice.

"Can you think of anyone who might have a reason to hurt you?" Lane asked.

Chelsea shook her head. "No, no one." She looked searchingly at Johnny and then back at Lane. "I don't know why this is happening. I wish somebody could tell me why this is happening to me. I've racked my brain trying to figure out the who and the why."

Johnny walked over and sank down on the sofa beside her as Lane continued to question her. "And you saw no identifying features on the person."

"None. He had on a ski mask and was wearing dark clothes," she replied.

"When he reached through the window, what was the color of his skin?" Lane continued.

"He was wearing gloves. I didn't see any of his skin."

Even though Johnny was several inches away from her, he could still feel the tremors of her body. Tears clung to her incredibly long eyelashes, and her face was as pale as he'd ever seen it.

A surge of protectiveness rose up inside him, along with a healthy dose of anger. He wanted to find the person who was tormenting her and beat the man's face in. He also wanted to pull Chelsea tight against him and hold her until her tremors of fear halted. However, he remained where he was as Lane continued to question her.

Lane was a good lawman, but no matter how good he was he couldn't find a bad guy without any clues, and so far it sounded like there were none at all.

Since the perp had worn gloves, then there would be no fingerprints. Since he'd worn a ski mask, there would be no physical description. How was Lane supposed to catch a ghost who struck at night and left no evidence behind? And who on earth would want to hurt Chelsea?

"What about back in New York? Was there anyone there who was giving you trouble?" Lane asked.

She frowned. "Actually there were two people I had to get a restraining order against," she said, surprising Johnny. "I'm not sure if either of them was truly dangerous, but they were definitely super-fan stalkers that made me frightened."

"What are their names?" Lane asked.

"Jerry Walkins and Dixie Sampson."

As Lane gathered more information on those two people, another thought suddenly flittered through Johnny's brain. Surely it wasn't possible. "Chelsea? Is it possible the attacker was a woman?" he asked.

She looked at him in surprise. "I guess anything is possible. Why would you ask that?"

"I just figured if we could rule out a woman being responsible, then it would make the investigation easier for Lane," he replied.

She frowned and looked at Lane. "I'm sorry. I don't know if it was a man or a woman. I don't know if he was black or white or green." Her voice rose with a touch of hysteria. "I don't know who or why or anything."

"Chelsea, it's important that you tell me if you think of anyone you might have accidentally offended or hurt," Lane said. "Maybe before you left town you said or did something to hurt somebody, and now that you've returned to town they want to make you pay."

"The only person I hurt before I left town was Johnny." She looked at him now, her eyes filled with guilt and what appeared to be regret.

"I'm certainly not the bad guy here," he protested.

"I didn't mean that," Chelsea replied hurriedly. "My point is that before I left here I don't believe I hurt or angered anyone except you, and I know you would never do anything like this to me."

Lane put his small notebook into his back pocket. "My guys have cleared the area and didn't see anyone lurking around the house or in the general neighborhood. Whoever it is, he's probably done for the night. Unfortunately, you'll need to replace some glass in your back door."

"I'll help her with that," Johnny said and got up from the sofa.

"Chelsea, I'll be in touch," Lane said. The two other patrol officers left, and then Johnny stepped outside with Lane.

"Well, I think we now know that the chase across your pasture was about Chelsea and not your family," Lane said when the two men stepped out into the darkness of night. "And I have serious doubts that somebody followed her here from New York. I would have noticed a new face in town."

"I agree. This might sound crazy, but maybe you should check out Tanya for this," Johnny said.

From the light of the streetlamp, Johnny saw the surprise that flittered across Lane's face. "Tanya... really? You think this might be some sort of a jealousy issue?"

"Hell if I know, but it's possible Tanya might see Chelsea as some sort of a rival. The two never really got along in the past. I can't see Tanya doing something like this, but I also can't think of anyone else who might have a motive to hurt Chelsea."

"I'll check her out," Lane said. "And in the meantime, call me if you think of anything else."

"Will do." Johnny watched as the chief headed to his car, and then he went back inside where Chelsea was still on the sofa. "I'm going to go into the kitchen and check things out."

Chelsea nodded, and he went in to see what the

person had done. The door had panes of glass, and two of them had been broken in the effort to reach in and unlock the door.

A slight chill walked up his spine. If Chelsea hadn't awakened when she had, the person would have been inside the house. He didn't even want to think about what might have happened.

There was no way he would believe that this person didn't mean to harm Chelsea. It would have been so damned easy to overtake her while she was sleeping. Another chill swept through him.

He returned to the living room and sank back down next to Chelsea. He was grateful to see that some of the color had returned to her face, although her eyes were still filled with more than a little bit of fear.

"Are you doing okay now?" he asked, even though he knew she wasn't.

"Yes…no… I just don't understand any of this," she replied in obvious frustration. "I have no idea why this is happening to me. Who hates me enough to do these things to me?"

"I wish I had an answer to give you. Do you have anything around here I can use to board up the door with?"

She frowned. "There might be something out in the shed in the back. Jeb has brought in a few supplies to fix the porch, and I think there was already some scrap pieces of wood in there when I moved in."

"I'll go check it out. Do you have a flashlight?"

"There's one under the kitchen sink." She got up from the sofa, and together they returned to the kitchen. When she saw the door, tears once again welled up in her eyes.

Johnny couldn't help but respond. He pulled her into his arms once again. "Don't cry, Chelsea. The good news is you're safe now."

"Yeah, but the bad news is the person is still somewhere out there," she replied.

"And tomorrow you'll go out and buy some extra locks. You also might consider contacting Charlie Harrison down at the feed store. He carries and installs a line of home alarm systems." He released her and got the large flashlight out from beneath the sink. "I'll be back in just a few minutes."

"I'll just stand right here and wait for you."

He opened the door, stepped outside and then clicked on the flashlight's high beam while she moved to stand on the threshold.

He shone the flashlight to the left and then the right as he headed toward the large shed in the back. Back and forth he checked out the surroundings. He saw nothing to give him pause. He almost hoped he'd see somebody hiding in the night shadows. More than anything he wanted to find the person responsible for Chelsea's terror-filled eyes and her fearful cries.

Once inside the shed he found a piece of scrap plywood big enough to cover over the broken windowpanes. Now, he hoped she had a hammer and some nails.

He found what he needed in a large bucket of tools Jeb had left behind, and it took him only minutes to hammer the plywood into place while she swept up all the broken glass. "Now nobody is getting through here," he said to Chelsea when he was finished.

"I'm still so afraid." She wrapped her arms around herself and hesitated a long moment and then spoke again. "Johnny, I know it's a lot to ask, but would you consider staying with me for the rest of the night? Please? I wouldn't ask if I wasn't so freaked out."

Her eyes pleaded with him, and she looked so small and fragile he couldn't help but say yes even as warning bells rang in the back of his mind.

He'd spent the last ten days staying away from her, not wanting to care deeply about her ever again. But there was no way he'd walk away from her now when she was so frightened and needed somebody… needed him to make her feel safe through the rest of the night.

"Okay, I'll stay," he told her.

"Thank you, Johnny. I really appreciate it."

Minutes later Johnny went around the house, checking to make sure all doors and windows were closed and locked up tight, and then he followed her up the stairs to her bedroom.

"Sorry about the mess," she said. "Jeb has been working in here."

"It's fine. At this time of the early morning, the most important thing now is getting some sleep," he replied.

She nodded and crawled into bed while he took off his gun belt and his shirt and then shucked his jeans, leaving him clad only in his boxers.

He got into bed next to her, and she immediately curled herself against his side. It felt only natural that his arm would wrap around her as she cuddled closer against him. "Thank you, Johnny," she murmured sleepily. "I feel so much better with you here next to me."

"Just go to sleep," he returned softly. It didn't take long until her slow, deep breathing let him know she'd fallen asleep. He wasn't so lucky.

Each point of contact where their skin met felt fevered. The familiar scent of her evoked memories of making love to her, and those memories tormented him.

While there had been a few women he had slept with since she'd left town, Tanya wasn't one of them. He enjoyed her company, but didn't have a sense of deep desire for her.

There had only ever been one woman he'd had deep desire for, and that was the woman curled up next to him, her soft breathing warming the base of his throat. Even now, not wanting to feel anything for her, he couldn't help the sweeping passion, the deep caring that rose up inside him for her.

Of course, he didn't love her. He refused to ever love her again, but that didn't stop him from wanting her. But he didn't intend to ever return there with her. He instinctively knew that to act on his physical desire for her would give her the wrong message. There was no future for them together. She had to know that he would never put his heart on the line for her again.

He consciously slowed his breathing and watched the shadow of the tree outside her window dance along the ceiling. Finally, he fell asleep and into sweet dreams of Chelsea.

Chapter Six

Chelsea awoke slowly. She was wrapped in warmth, spooned against Johnny's body. His arm was thrown across her waist and his even breathing whispered against her nape.

Oh, how she had missed this. How she had missed him. The moment he had walked into her house last night, she'd felt safe and protected, like it was right for him to be here with her.

She was so grateful he'd agreed to stay with her overnight. Despite the terror she'd experienced earlier in the night, she had slept soundly and peacefully in his arms. She knew if he hadn't been there, she would have gotten no sleep at all. She'd always slept peacefully in Johnny's arms.

She now slowly extricated herself from his embrace and turned over, grateful that her movements hadn't awakened him. With a faint glow of morning sneaking in around her curtains, she stared at his features.

Even in sleep and with a five-o'clock shadow dusting his lower jaw, he looked beautiful and strong. His brow was smooth, and his brown eyelashes were dark, thick and long. His sexy mouth was relaxed, and all she could think about was kissing him.

She didn't know how long she had been looking at him when his eyes suddenly opened and he was looking back at her. In the depths of his eyes was a flame that instantly lit a fire deep inside her. "Johnny." His name fell from her lips on a whisper of want…of need and she placed a hand on his chest.

"Chelsea," he whispered back. He looked still half-asleep as his arms reached out to pull her closer to him.

And then her lips were on his in a kiss that erased any other thoughts from her head. There was just Johnny and his sexy lips stoking the heat inside her even hotter.

His hands began to move up and down her back in slow caresses that half stole her breath away. This was where she belonged, in Johnny's big, strong arms. This was where she had always belonged.

He deepened the kiss, his tongue swirling erotically with hers. It felt wonderfully comfortable and familiar and yet exciting and different. It had been so long since she'd been kissed by him, so long since she'd been held in his arms.

For five years she'd longed for him. For five long

years she'd yearned for him. It hadn't been just this she had missed. She'd ached for the conversations they used to have about both serious and silly things. She'd wanted to hear his deep laughter and for five years had only imagined it in her mind.

His hands now moved to her breasts. Even through the cotton material of her nightshirt, his touch caused electrical currents to zing through her, and her nipples rose eagerly.

She sat up and pulled her nightshirt over her head, leaving her clad only in a pair of wispy pink panties. She then crawled on top of him. His hands immediately covered her breasts once again. Warm and slightly calloused, his hands not only cupped her but also teased and tormented her turgid peaks.

She could feel his erection beneath her. He was fully aroused, and that only turned her on more. He had to feel the same way about her that she did about him. Surely he forgave her for the past and knew they belonged together from this amazing moment forward.

She moved her hips against him, and he moaned deep in his throat. She leaned over and kissed him at the base of his throat. She then licked and kissed up his neck to just behind his ear.

He moaned again. God, she loved the sound of his pleasure. He pulled her down, and their lips reconnected in a kiss of desperate need and sweet, hot desire. Within moments his boxers and her panties were off, and they were skin-to-skin.

He lifted her up and positioned her to take him in. She knew he'd always liked her to be on the top, and as she eased down on him, she released a low moan. For a moment she didn't move as she waited for her body to adjust to his length. He filled her up in an exquisite way.

Then she moved, raising herself up and then sinking back down on him. He hissed his pleasure, and his eyes burned into hers. She felt as if he was making love to her with his eyes, those blue eyes that appeared to be looking into her very soul.

He placed his hands on either side of her, and she leaned forward and popped her hips faster, pleasuring herself at the same time she pleasured him.

"Chelsea." He whispered her name with tremendous emotion, the single word filled with desire and love.

"Johnny, my sweet Johnny," she whispered back. Her body was filled with him, as was her mind. There was nothing but him and her and this moment.

Her climax was suddenly on her, shooting wave after wave of intense fulfillment through her. At the same time he moaned her name again and then groaned with his own release.

She collapsed on top of him, gasping with breathless joy. He too was winded for several minutes. When her breathing finally returned to normal, she remained on his chest.

The room was quiet except for the soft tapping of tree limbs against her window. "I can't believe you found a house with a big tree outside your bedroom window."

She laughed softly. "If it wasn't for that big tree outside my bedroom window while I was growing up, I wouldn't have been able to sneak out to meet you."

"Have you climbed down the one here yet?" he asked.

"Not yet. Want to do it with me?" She raised her head to look at him.

"I know you've got to be teasing me because you know I don't do heights," he replied.

She smiled. "I'm definitely teasing you." She straightened up and smiled down at him.

"I know what you want now," she said.

"And what would that be?" he asked.

"Some of my super special French toast with a big side of bacon," she replied.

"You really don't have to cook for me, Chelsea," he protested.

"Of course I don't have to, but I really want to," she replied. "I know you always liked my French toast. Please let me make it for you as a thank-you for staying here with me last night."

He smiled up at her. "Okay, go knock yourself out."

She crawled off him, grabbed clothes out of her closet and then headed for the bathroom. A few minutes later she went down the stairs to the kitchen. She refused to allow the sight of her back door boarded up to spoil the happiness that flooded through her veins in this moment.

Her body still felt warm from Johnny's, and her heart was filled with the knowledge that he still wanted her...that he must still love her. She put the coffee on to brew, then grabbed a frying pan and got the bacon going.

Everything had happened so quickly. Their passion had been like a sweeping wildfire that had raged quickly out of control. That's how it had always been between them, and she was happy that nothing about that had changed.

She knew Johnny would probably leave once he ate. She couldn't expect him to hang around all day. He had ranch business to get back to, and she needed to head to the feed store and talk to Charlie Harrison about getting a security system. But right now the sun was shining, and she wanted to keep this happiness she felt about her relationship with Johnny going.

By the time the bacon was finished frying and she'd pulled out her griddle to make the French toast, Johnny joined her in the kitchen. Although he was clad in the same clothes, she could tell he'd taken a shower. He smelled fresh and clean, and his hair was damp and shiny.

She wished she had known he was going to

shower. She would have loved to join him and wind up in bed once again for another bout of lovemaking.

"Sit down and I'll pour you a cup of coffee," she said.

He sank down at the table. "I didn't get a chance to tell you last night, but I can't believe how you've pulled this place together so quickly."

"It's been with a lot of help from Jeb. Thanks for giving me his contact information. He's fast but thorough, and I'm really pleased with his work so far." She carried a cup of coffee to him and then went back to the counter to finish up the French toast.

There had been many mornings in their past when he would show up at her mother's back door, and Chelsea would pull him inside and make him breakfast. This felt natural; it felt so right for her to be cooking him the morning meal once again.

As she worked, they talked about the house, not only the things she'd already accomplished but the things she still wanted to do.

While they ate breakfast, she was grateful that the conversation remained light and neither of them spoke about the events from the night before that had brought him here with her. She didn't even want to think about the terror she'd felt when she'd seen the intruder at her back door.

"I'll help you with the dishes," he said once the meal was finished.

"You don't have to do that," she protested.

"I always helped clean up after breakfast so we didn't leave a mess for your mother to be upset about," he replied.

She smiled ruefully. "Even when we left the kitchen spotless, she always found something to complain about."

He rose and grabbed their plates as she got up and reached for the syrup and butter in the center of the table. He fell silent as they worked to clean up the kitchen.

"I've got to get back to the ranch," he said when they were finished with the work and they went into the living room. "But before I go, we need to have a talk. Why don't we sit for a minute?"

"Okay." She sat on the sofa, her heart suddenly beating too fast. He looked so serious. What did he want to talk about now?

He sat next to her, a frown appearing across his forehead. "Chelsea, I'm not lying when I say making love to you again was wonderful, but it was wrong."

"Wrong? What was wrong about it? Johnny, being back in your arms was positively magical."

He winced. "I'm sorry, but it shouldn't have happened, and it won't happen again. I don't want to give you the wrong idea, Chelsea. We had our time together, and it ended five years ago. We didn't work out, and our time is over. I'm just not willing to try it again."

She stared at him as each one of his words

chipped away at her happiness and stabbed her through her heart. She still loved him but also realized she couldn't make him love her again. Given their past and the way she had left him, it was no wonder he wasn't willing to try again.

"Making love with you once certainly didn't make me think we were going to have a relationship." She said the lie around the large lump in her throat. "Don't worry, Johnny. I don't expect anything from you."

Relief smoothed out his frown, and he stood. "Thanks, Chelsea. I just needed to know that we're on the same page." He smiled at her. "Nevertheless, I certainly want you to contact me if anything else happens with whoever is after you."

She got up from the sofa, and together they walked to the front door. "Even though it's Sunday, I'm assuming I can talk to Charlie Harrison this afternoon about putting in a security system here."

"Good, that will certainly give me some peace of mind." He reached up and ran his hand down her cheek, and she couldn't help but turn into the caress. "I care about you, Chelsea," he said softly. "I'll always care about you, and I want to be here for you as a friend." He dropped his hand back to his side.

She forced her lips to turn up in a smile. "Thanks, Johnny, I appreciate that. I can always use another friend." She unlocked the door and opened it.

"Keep in touch, and I'll see you around," he said.

"Bye, Johnny." She watched as he walked down her sidewalk to his truck parked by the curb, then she closed and relocked the door and returned to the sofa.

She sank down, grabbed one of the throw pillows and held it tightly against her aching chest. She'd thought…she'd assumed…she'd just hoped that what they had just shared in bed meant they were back to where they had been before she'd left town.

She'd been foolish to believe that a passionate roll in bed would fix her relationship with him. She should have known it was much more complicated than that. She'd been stupid to believe that he would want to get back together with her.

Trying to hold in the tears that suddenly burned hot at her eyes, she mentally kicked herself for being upset. Yet she was upset. She felt as if the rug had been pulled out from under her. Until this very moment, she hadn't realized how much she'd wanted to be loved by Johnny again.

He wanted to be here for her as a friend. Had any woman in love ever heard worse words? She lost the battle with her tears, and they began to trek down her cheeks as the reality of her situation pounded in her head.

And the reality was she loved a man who would never love her back and she had a person who appeared to want her dead.

JOHNNY MENTALLY KICKED himself as he got into his truck to head home from Chelsea's house. He chastised himself for being so weak where Chelsea was concerned.

He'd known the moment he'd opened his eyes that she wanted to make love to him. He'd recognized the hunger in her eyes as he'd seen it a thousand times in their past.

There was no question that in that moment she had stirred a white-hot desire in him. What he should have done was immediately get out of bed and head home.

Instead, he'd given in to his own desire. And it had been just as wonderful, just as magical, as it had always been with her. Maybe someplace in the back of his mind, he'd hoped it wouldn't be as good as he remembered. But that hadn't been the case.

Her lips had tasted like they always had, of exciting first love and hot summer caresses. She had tasted of cold snuggly nights and the hope of love forever more.

Holding her in his arms again had been like a dream come true. She'd fit so neatly against him, like she always had. For the past five years he had tried to forget the passion he'd always had for her, but making love to her again had only reminded him of his wild and deep desire for her.

And the minute she had placed his breakfast on the table before him, he'd realized she wanted to get back with him, that she wanted to go back to when they were together and happy. He'd seen it in the shine of her eyes, in the soft smiles that had curved her lips.

He knew he'd hurt her. Despite her brave face, he'd seen the signs on her features. He should take pleasure in that, given how badly she had hurt him in the past, but he didn't. He was surprised to realize that the very last thing he would ever want to do was hurt Chelsea, no matter what had happened in their past.

He had shared some of the best moments of his life with her. She knew him better than anyone else on this earth knew him. She knew he had an irrational fear of heights and that he dreamed of having a big family.

She knew that he'd wet his pants in the third grade, and instead of telling anyone, he had run out of the classroom and all the way home. He'd hidden in the barn until his father had found him. She knew things he'd never shared with anyone else.

Now he knew how important it was that he stay away from her. Because he had no desire to go back in time and rekindle a relationship with her, the kindest thing he could do for her and for himself was stay out of her life.

He hoped Lane figured out who was after her. He also hoped Lane would figure out who killed his father, but at the moment, the most imminent danger was to Chelsea.

Minutes later when he pulled up in front of his cabin, he was surprised to see Luke sitting in one of the chairs outside his front door.

"Hey, brother. What's up?" he asked when he got out of his truck.

"You tell me what's up," Luke said, a slightly hostile tone to his voice.

Johnny got his house key out and frowned at his brother. "What's chapping your hide this morning?"

Luke looked left and then right and then got up from the chair. "Let's talk inside."

The two men entered the cabin, and Johnny gestured his brother to the sofa while he sank down in his recliner. "What's going on with you this morning?"

Luke leaned forward and drummed his fingers briefly on the top of the coffee table. From the time Luke was a young boy he'd always been a tapper when he was nervous or upset.

"The real question is what's going on with you this morning?" Luke said with a raised brow.

"What are you talking about?" Johnny asked in confusion.

"I knew when she came back to town she'd be a major distraction for you. I'm assuming that's where you were last night…with her." Luke didn't even try to hide his irritation.

Johnny released a dry laugh. "I haven't had to explain my whereabouts to anybody for a very long time. But yes, I was with Chelsea." Johnny went on to explain the call he'd received from her in the middle of the night and what had happened.

When he was finished, Luke looked a bit contrite. "I'm sorry she's going through something like that. Does Lane have any ideas who might be after her?"

Johnny shook his head. "None."

"Lane is batting zero right now with figuring out what's going on in this town." A simmering anger was back in Luke's voice. "I just don't want you to get all caught up in Chelsea and forget that somebody killed Dad."

"First of all, I'm not about to forget that Dad was murdered, and second, you don't have to worry about me getting 'all caught up in Chelsea' because I don't intend to have a relationship with her. But if I did decide to date her, then it wouldn't be any of your business," Johnny replied firmly.

Luke flushed. "Johnny, it's been almost a month, and we aren't any closer to getting answers about his murder. I'm just so damned frustrated. I feel like each day that passes without answers is a dishonor to Dad."

"What do you suggest we do, Luke?"

Luke ran a hand through his shaggy dark hair and a deep frown creased his forehead. "I think it's time we start our own investigation."

"I've given Lane every name of anyone I could think of who might have a motive. I even told him to look at Caleb. What else can we do?"

"I still think it was either Wayne Bridges or Joe Daniels who did it. Both of them were running against Dad in the mayoral race, and they both knew Dad was beating them by a lot."

"I agree, but how do we investigate them better than Lane already has?"

"I don't know," Luke admitted. His eyes held a torment that Johnny had never seen there before. "I just feel like I need to do something."

"Luke, the best thing we can do right now is leave the investigation to Lane and his staff. We have a ranch to run here, and I need you to be focused on being my right-hand man."

Luke nodded slowly, the frown still running across his face. "I just feel like I'm letting down Dad by not doing anything more."

"You aren't letting down Dad," Johnny countered. "If we let the ranch business fall apart, then we'd be letting him down."

Luke drew a deep breath and released it. "I know you're right. And speaking of that, I guess I'll get back to the chores." He got up from the sofa and Johnny stood as well.

When they reached the door, Johnny patted his brother on the back. "We're all hurting, Luke, but we need to leave things to Lane and his officers and wait for justice to be served."

"My biggest fear is that we aren't going to ever get any answers. We'll never know who killed him, and the murderer will still be walking the streets of our town."

"Yeah, that's my fear too," Johnny admitted as the two stepped outside. "Just don't get too deep into your head, Luke. You know you've always had a tendency to do that."

"I know." Luke flashed him a quick grin. "Sorry if I ruined your morning with all this."

Johnny returned his smile. "Hey, no harm, no foul. Come on, I'll walk with you to the stable, and we can take a ride together through the cattle."

"Sounds good to me."

The brothers saddled up and rode together for an hour and a half, talking about pasture grass and the general health of the cattle and checking water troughs to make sure they were all full.

Then they parted ways. Johnny headed back to the cabin to check inventory and cut payroll checks for the men who worked for them, and Luke rode on to check the condition of some of the farther pastures.

It took Johnny most of the afternoon to write checks and contact suppliers to order various items that the ranch needed. It took longer than usual because thoughts of Chelsea kept intruding in his mind.

Had she contacted Charlie about a security system? Had she installed more locks on her doors? He couldn't help but be concerned about her after what had happened the night before. No matter how many times he told himself she wasn't his problem, he couldn't stop worrying about her.

He finally knocked off work to have dinner with his family. Caleb didn't show up, nor did Ashley, who was working late at her store. It was a quiet meal with just his mother, Luke and himself.

As he was walking back to his cabin he saw Caleb standing just outside the barn with Leroy and deep in conversation. They were near two fifty-gallon drums that held special feed for a couple of the horses. Once again, he wondered what the two had in common. It was definitely an odd friendship as far as Johnny was concerned, but just like his relationship with Chelsea wasn't any of Luke's business, Caleb's friendship wasn't any of Johnny's business.

The minute he got back into the cabin, he picked up the phone and called Tanya. "Hi, Johnny." Her voice was warm and welcoming.

"Hey, Tanya. How are you doing?"

"I'm just finishing up some lesson plans for school tomorrow," she replied. Tanya was a third-grade teacher at the local elementary school. "What are you doing?"

"I've spent most of the day doing paperwork," he replied.

"Ugh. Don't you hate wasting a beautiful spring day with admin?"

"I do, but it's a necessary evil. I was actually wondering if this Friday night you'd like to have dinner with me at the café and then head to the Red Barn for a little two-stepping?"

"Sounds like a perfect way to end a week. I'd love to go with you," she replied.

"Great, why don't I pick you up around six?"

"That will be just fine. Anything else new?" she asked.

He immediately wondered if she'd heard he'd spent the night at Chelsea's place. It would only take one person driving by and seeing his truck parked there early this morning for word to get back to Tanya.

He decided to tell her the truth, minus the intimate details that really weren't anyone's business. He wasn't sleeping with Tanya, so he hadn't broken any sacred trust. They also had never talked about theirs being a monogamous dating relationship.

Still, he told her about the attempted break-in there and that he'd spent the night, although he didn't tell her he'd passed it in Chelsea's bed.

"Oh my goodness, that's terrible," Tanya said when he was finished. "I'm just glad she's okay."

It was obvious from her surprise at the news that Lane hadn't spoken to her yet. "She should be just fine," he said. "She planned on getting extra locks today and finding out about a security system."

"That's good. Still, it's hard to believe those things are even necessary in Coyote Creek. Do the police know who's responsible?"

"Lane had no idea last night, and I haven't heard anything more from him today. It's really not my issue," he replied firmly, as if trying to convince himself of that fact.

"Well, I hope Lane finds the bad guy."

"Me too, but that's between Chelsea and Lane. So, we're all set for Friday night?"

"Definitely. I look forward to it."

They said their goodbyes, and then Johnny took off his gun belt and settled into his chair to relax and watch some television.

His call to Tanya had been an attempt to get Chelsea out of his mind. It didn't work as well as he'd hoped. Thoughts of Chelsea and what they had shared continued to run through his brain.

He must have dozed off, for the sound of gunshots jerked him awake and out of his chair. What the hell? As more gunfire boomed, he grabbed his gun from the holster and headed for the front door.

He must have dozed longer than he'd thought, as deep twilight had fallen. Still, he was able to see

Caleb and Leroy pinned behind the gallon drums by gunfire coming from two, possibly three, men in the distance.

He saw Leroy returning fire, but he knew Caleb probably didn't have a weapon with him. He rarely carried a gun even when he was out and about the ranch. Johnny slid out his cabin door.

As the men in the field continued to shoot toward Caleb and Leroy, Johnny began shooting toward them. Luke appeared next to Johnny and added his firepower to Johnny's.

The men in the distance suddenly disappeared, and the night went still. "What is going on?" Luke asked, breaking the silence that had descended.

"Hell if I know. I heard the gunshots and came out here to see what was going on. Maybe Caleb can fill us in." With one eye on the place where the shooters had been, Johnny walked hurriedly to the barn with Luke by his side.

Caleb and Leroy stepped out from behind the drums. "Thanks for the help," Leroy said with a cautious look toward the field.

"Either of you two want to fill us in on what's going on?" Johnny asked, his gaze going from Leroy to Caleb.

"We don't know," Caleb replied. "We were just hanging around out here, and all of a sudden those men appeared and started shooting at us."

"Did you recognize any of them?" Luke asked.

"Yeah, did you know who they were?" Johnny added.

Leroy and Caleb exchanged quick glances. "I have no idea who they were," Caleb replied.

"I didn't recognize any of them. It all happened too fast," Leroy said.

Johnny frowned, unsure if he believed them or not. "Have you two had trouble with anyone? Offended somebody?"

"Not me," Caleb said quickly. "I haven't even left the ranch in the last couple of weeks."

"I haven't had any trouble with anyone either. I've been keeping my nose to the grindstone at the Blacks' during the day and hanging out here with Caleb in the evenings," Leroy said.

"And you're positive you didn't recognize any of them," Johnny pressed.

The two men looked at each other and then back at Johnny. Both of them indicated they had no idea who the men were, but Johnny didn't believe them. There had to be a reason that somebody had been shooting at them.

Or had this been an attempt to take out another member of the King family?

"I'm going to drive up there and see if I can find anything that might give us a clue about them," Johnny said.

"I'll go with you," Luke replied.

"Do you think this was an attack on our family?" Luke asked minutes later when they were in Johnny's truck and headed toward the area where the men had been when they'd been firing their guns.

"Maybe," Johnny said. "I suppose it's possible that whoever shot Dad isn't done with us yet. However, I got the feeling Leroy and Caleb weren't telling us the whole truth about not knowing who the men were."

"The real question is what mess the two of them might be in," Luke said.

"I honestly don't know what to think about this," Johnny admitted.

He drove as far as he could into the field and then parked the truck, and the two brothers got out and walked to where Johnny thought the men had stood shooting. With the aid of powerful flashlights from Johnny's cabin, they began to scan the area.

Johnny shone his light in the distance where trees crowded together and the brush was thick and tangled. This was a field they didn't use because of the rise and fall of the land and the heavy woods.

Seeing nothing amiss, he continued his search on the ground. "The grass is trampled in patterns that could only be made by horses," he said.

"So, whoever it was, they rode in," Luke replied.

"It looks like it." Johnny tightened his hand around

his flashlight. Was this really just another attack on his family, or was Caleb harboring secrets…dark secrets that could potentially get them all killed?

Chapter Seven

It had been another busy week for Chelsea. She'd bought herself a car, a midsize Ford that was bright red and had low mileage. She'd spent a day driving around on country roads, making turns left and right to familiarize herself after five years of not driving any kind of a vehicle.

It was Friday, and tonight she was going to the Red Barn with Melinda and Roger, although she'd insisted that she would meet the couple at the local bar. She knew they'd want to stay much later than she did so it was important she have her own set of wheels to come home in when she'd had enough of the loud music and socializing.

However, that was later tonight. Before the night's activity, her mother was coming over for lunch. It would be the first time her mother would be visiting her here, and Chelsea wanted everything to be perfect.

She checked the table, pleased with the fresh flower arrangement she'd bought earlier in the day.

The water glasses were spotless, and her yellow dishes with the yellow-and-white-checkered cloth napkins looked cheerful and bright.

The chicken salad was in the refrigerator, ready to be placed on the croissant rolls, and a large green salad awaited drizzling with homemade green goddess dressing. There was also cherry cheesecake from her mother's favorite bakery in town for dessert.

Jeb had continued to work on the house. He'd finished up the painting in her bedroom, and she had set him to work on the porch steps and railing before painting more inside. He'd finished the work on them late last night. He had three more rooms to paint upstairs, and then the entire outside of the house.

Charlie Harrison had sent several men to her place to install a security system, so she now felt safe in her own home. It had been a good week except for one thing...the absence of Johnny.

Even though she knew she needed to get over him, that there was no path forward for her with him, it was difficult to do. While her head had gotten his message loud and clear, her heart still refused to let go.

However, she couldn't think about him now, not with her mother arriving within minutes. She did one last run-through to make sure everything was dusted and clean, and by that time her mother was knocking on her door.

"Hi, come in," Chelsea greeted her mother with a smile.

"The place is a bit of an eyesore," Stella said with a frown.

"Jeb will be painting it all in the next couple of days," Chelsea replied. "Why don't you have a seat on the sofa so we can visit for a while. It seems like it has been forever since I've seen or talked to you." Chelsea gestured toward the sofa.

"Can't we just get right to lunch? I have a lot of things to do today, and I shouldn't be taking this time off as it is," Stella asked.

"Of course. Then come on into the kitchen. It will just take me a matter of minutes to get the meal on the table." Chelsea led her mother into the kitchen where Stella sat and gazed around. Chelsea got busy pulling things out of the fridge.

"It looks good in here," Stella said. "The fresh flowers on the table are a nice touch."

"Thanks. I thought you might enjoy them." Chelsea dressed the salad and then placed it on the table and then quickly put together the chicken croissants. After filling their glasses with ice and water, she then sat down across from her mother.

"Word on the street is you're definitely in position to become the next mayor," Chelsea said.

"Big John King had a good platform, and by me

espousing the same values and goals he had for this town, I'm capturing the votes that would have gone to him."

"Maybe as mayor you can do something to help find his killer," Chelsea said.

"That would be nice, wouldn't it? I heard through the grapevine that you had a little excitement here too. Somebody tried to break in?"

"It was the same man who chased me through the pasture," Chelsea said.

Stella's nostrils thinned, and her lip curled up. "I'm sure whoever tried to break in here was hoping to get a stash of new items knowing that you'd just moved in."

"Maybe," Chelsea replied. The last thing she wanted was to get into an argument with her mother about what had happened. But Chelsea knew that the man trying to break in hadn't wanted any stash of new items. He'd wanted to hurt her…possibly kill her.

"Well, there's only a couple more weeks before the election. What all do you have planned to assure your success?" Chelsea asked, knowing her mother loved to talk about herself.

Stella lit up, and for the rest of the meal she talked about town-hall meetings and campaign gatherings and what she intended to do as mayor of the small town.

Once Stella was finished eating, she rose and

headed for the front door. Chelsea had bagged up the cheesecake as her mother was taking the dessert with her. "Thank you for the meal. It was quite good, I must say. And I'll really enjoy the cheesecake later this evening."

"I'm so glad you enjoyed the meal," Chelsea replied.

"I'm glad it looks like you're settling in here nicely. Now, if you could just find a man for yourself."

Chelsea smiled. "I could say the same thing to you."

"I have never needed a man in my life, but you're weak, Chelsea. And you're young. You need a man to give me some grandbabies. I still can't believe you screwed things up so badly with Johnny."

"I guess Johnny wasn't written in the stars for me," Chelsea replied and couldn't help the sadness that laced her voice.

"Ah, I hear the regret in your voice. Unfortunately, we all have to live with the consequences of the choices we make in life. For me, my one regret was sleeping with your father. I knew he was no good, but he was a handsome, smooth-talking devil, and I let down my guard. Then the moment I told him I was pregnant, he ran for the hills or back to hell where he belonged."

It was a story Chelsea had heard for most of her

life, and she believed it was at the root of why her mother didn't really love her.

Stella had been married to Jacob's father, but when Jacob was just a baby, Greg Black had died in a tragic farm accident. Stella had loved Greg, and she adored their son, but there had been far less love for the little girl whose father had abandoned her mother.

After Stella left, Chelsea cleaned up the kitchen and then went upstairs for a short nap before the night out. She awoke at five thirty, ate a leftover chicken croissant and then headed back upstairs to start getting ready for the night. She was meeting Melinda and Roger at seven in front of the popular bar.

The Red Barn was strictly casual, so Chelsea pulled on a pair of jeans and a fitted red blouse that hung just off her shoulders. She put her makeup on a little heavier, adding color to her cheeks and then focusing on her eyes.

When she was ready, it was time to go. She grabbed her house keys and set the alarm, then headed toward her car in the driveway.

As she drove toward the outskirts of town where the bar was located, she found herself thinking about the lunch with her mother. It had gone far better than Chelsea had expected. Maybe with Chelsea living separately but in the same town with her mother, they could build a new and better relationship. Chelsea certainly hoped so. She'd always longed for a loving relationship with her mother.

However, Chelsea wasn't weak, and she certainly didn't need a man to complete her. She had gone through some of the worst days of her life at the end of her stay in New York, and she'd gone through it all alone.

Needing a man and wanting one were two different things. She wanted Johnny, but she didn't need him. She wanted him, and he didn't want her.

She released a deep sigh. Maybe she'd meet somebody tonight who would spark her interest, somebody who would be interested in getting to know her. It would be nice to have somebody to share a meal with or spend an evening with.

As she drove, she told herself she needed to be open to meeting new people and reacquainting herself with others. She'd always been so wound up with Johnny she had never given other men in town a second look.

When she pulled up, the parking lot was already filling up. She saw Roger's truck and pulled into the empty space next to it. Melinda waved at her from Roger's passenger window.

They got out of their vehicles, and Melinda grabbed Chelsea's arm. "I was afraid you wouldn't come," she said.

"Well, I'm here," Chelsea replied. As she looked

toward the large building with neon beer signs flashing in the windows, a wave of nervousness struck her.

She hadn't put herself out there in such a public forum since she'd returned to Coyote Creek. Would people believe the press that had excoriated her? Would they believe she was a drug addict who had self-destructed? Or a woman with mental issues? Would she be treated like a pariah? Would nobody be interested in approaching her?

"Come on, Chelsea. You'll be just fine," Melinda said as if she'd read Chelsea's mind.

"We're here for you," Roger added.

"Thanks. You're right, I'll be just fine," Chelsea replied firmly in an attempt to assure not only them but herself.

"Then let's get inside and get a table." Melinda headed toward the entrance with Chelsea and Roger trailing behind. Stepping inside the dim interior was like walking into another universe.

The air smelled of booze and greasy bar food, and the music piping in overhead was loud as peanut shells on the floor crunched underfoot.

Melinda led them to an empty table next to the large dance floor where several couples were already two-stepping to the country tune.

"What do you want to drink?" Roger asked her.

"Just a diet cola for me," Chelsea said.

"Nonsense," Melinda immediately said to Roger. "Get her a margarita, frozen like mine."

Chelsea started to protest but then decided to let Melinda have her way. Besides, it wouldn't hurt for Chelsea to have one drink while it was so early in the evening.

By the time Roger returned from the long bar on one side of the room, the place had grown more crowded. A blond man approached their table. He looked familiar to Chelsea, but his name escaped her.

"Chelsea." He greeted her with a wide, pleasant smile.

"Hi, Adam," Roger said, and instantly Chelsea remembered: Adam Pearson. He'd been in her high-school class and had always been nice to her.

"Hey, Adam," she now said. "How's it going?"

"Good, and it's great to see you back in town again. Would you take a turn on the dance floor with me?"

Chelsea hesitated for a long moment, and then Melinda unceremoniously pushed her off her chair. "She would love to dance with you, Adam," Melinda said.

Chelsea laughed. "I guess we're going to dance."

She and Adam moved to the large dance floor and began to dance to the rock music playing now. Adam was a good dancer, and Chelsea felt herself letting loose a bit.

"You know, I had a major crush on you in high

school," he said to her as they walked back to her table.

"Really? I never knew that," she replied in surprise.

"A lot of guys were crushing on you back then, but nobody ever approached you because everybody was afraid of Johnny, and it was obvious you two were a strong couple," he said.

"Well, that was then, and this is now," she replied.

"So, if I was to work up the nerve to ask you out to dinner at the café one evening, would you be interested?" he asked.

"I don't know. I guess you'll have to work up the nerve to ask me and then we'll see," she replied. God, she was being flirtatious. She'd never flirted with anyone but Johnny. They exchanged numbers, and then Adam left her at the table and headed across the room to the bar.

"You could do much worse," Melinda said.

"Yeah, Adam is a good guy," Roger added.

But he isn't Johnny, a little voice whispered in her head. "I'm open to getting to know him better," Chelsea finally replied.

"That's my girl," Melinda exclaimed.

Over the next half an hour, Chelsea was surprised by how many men invited her to dance with them. She exchanged numbers with several of them, hoping that maybe she could move on from Johnny. She had to open herself up in order to possibly have a new love.

As the night went on, she and Melinda and Roger shared a lot of laughs. Chelsea finished her drink and then ordered a diet cola, knowing another alcoholic drink might make her too buzzed to drive home safely.

She was surprised by how much fun she was having, and then he walked in, Johnny with Tanya by his side, and Chelsea's heart plummeted to the ground.

HE SAW HER almost immediately. Chelsea looked totally hot in her tight jeans and the red blouse that exposed her beautiful shoulders. Dammit, he couldn't help the way his heart leaped at the sight of her.

Tanya must have seen her too, for she grabbed Johnny's arm and held tight. He smiled down at the dark-haired woman. "Let's find a table, and I'll get our drinks," he said, raising his voice to be heard over the loud music.

It took only minutes to wind through the crowd and claim one of the few empty tables that were left. Unfortunately, the table gave him a perfect view of Chelsea and her friends at their table.

He got Tanya settled in and then wove his way back toward the bar. He was greeted by friends and acquaintances on his way. When he got to the bar, he ordered himself a whiskey on the rocks, and for Tanya he ordered a gin and tonic with a twist of lime. He'd been dating Tanya long enough to know what she liked.

Once he returned to the table, he pulled Tanya out on the dance floor. The fast-paced music couldn't get Chelsea out of his head. Even when the music slowed and Tanya was dancing close to him, it did nothing but make him remember all the times he had danced with Chelsea.

What the hell was wrong with him? He hadn't been able to get Chelsea out of his mind since they had made love again. Even now, memories of the two of them kept crashing through his head.

He saw Chelsea was dancing with Adam Pearson. Adam was a nice guy, but he was all wrong for her. Chelsea needed somebody who would challenge her mentally with stimulating conversation, somebody who was as passionate about things as she was. She needed somebody who shared the same quirky sense of humor. She needed somebody like him.

At that very moment he realized he needed to stop seeing Tanya. It was unfair of him to continue to date her knowing there was never going to be any kind of a future with her. He enjoyed her company, but he wasn't going to marry her. He was wasting her time, and that wasn't right.

He didn't know if there was any kind of a future with Chelsea, but she felt like unfinished business, and he wouldn't have complete closure where she was concerned unless he finished that business once and for all.

However, he needed to have the difficult conversation with Tanya tonight. Now that he realized she would never be his person, it seemed important he break it off with her as soon as possible. The last thing he wanted to do was keep her from finding a real love that would lead to marriage and children.

He knew the minute Chelsea left the bar, for she seemed to take all the color, all the vibrancy of the place, with her. She'd left alone, which made him ridiculously happy.

Melinda and Roger left soon after Chelsea. He and Tanya stayed another hour or so. Thankfully Tanya had only had the one alcoholic drink, so her mind should be clear for the conversation he'd have with her when he took her home.

All too soon he was pulling up in front of her attractive ranch house, and a ball of dread hung heavy in his stomach. He really should have done this long before now, and it had nothing to do with Chelsea returning to Coyote Creek.

"Want to come in for a nightcap?" Tanya asked when he cut his engine.

Several times after going out he ended the night with a drink at her place. He definitely didn't want to have his conversation with her in the car. He respected her far more than that.

"Okay, I'll come in for a few minutes," he replied.

Tanya lived in a modest ranch-style house a block off Main Street. Her living room was decorated in earth tones, making it feel warm and welcoming.

Once inside he declined the offer of another drink, and together they sat on the sofa.

"It was a fun evening. As always, thank you, Johnny," she said with a smile. It was a smile he knew he was about to knock off her lips.

"We need to talk, Tanya." Sure enough her smile instantly disappeared.

"You look quite serious," she observed.

"Tanya, I've really enjoyed the time we've spent together," he began. "But I'm sorry. I don't see our relationship proceeding any deeper, and dating me is really just a waste of your time."

Her brown eyes appeared to grow darker as she stared at him for a long moment. "It's her, isn't it?" A bitter laugh escaped her. "Of course it's her. I knew when she showed up back here in town she would ruin everything for us."

"This isn't about Chelsea and me, it is about us," he replied. "It's about me. I value your friendship, Tanya. But I don't see you as a romantic partner. I just don't have those kinds of feelings for you."

"Ah, so you're friend-zoning me." She raised one of her eyebrows and gazed at him with a hint of coldness in her eyes. "Have you slept with her yet?"

"That's really none of your business," he replied softly. "I'm sorry if I've hurt you. That was never my intention. I'd hoped that my feelings for you would move beyond caring about you into loving you, but that hasn't happened, and I don't believe it will."

Her gaze still held his, although she was utterly silent.

"Like I said, I'm really sorry, Tanya. I shouldn't have led you on for as long as I did."

"You're absolutely pathetic, Johnny," she said derisively. "You're still whipped over a woman who left you virtually at the altar. Chelsea is probably laughing over how easily she's wrapped you around her finger all over again."

Johnny winced and stood. "Tanya, I'd at least hoped we could still remain friends."

"Well, that's certainly not going to happen," she replied curtly. "You don't deserve my friendship."

"Then I'm sorry about that too," he said.

"Yeah, you're a sorry excuse of a man," she retorted. "You're a weasel, Johnny. I'm better for you than she will ever be. She's nothing but a joke, and you're an even bigger joke."

He headed for the door, refusing to sit and listen to her belittling words any longer. "Then I'll just say good-night now, and I'll see you around."

"Don't let the door hit you on your backside," she replied, the sarcasm still rife in her voice.

Johnny stepped out into the dark of the night and released a deep sigh. He knew he'd hurt Tanya, and he felt badly for that. Still, he'd been shocked by the vitriol in her voice, by the way she had responded to him. But he also felt a huge sense of relief.

With or without Chelsea being back in town, his

breakup with Tanya would have happened anyway. He'd dated Tanya long enough to know he was never going to fall in love with her, and Tanya had mentioned several times that she was looking forward to marriage and having children. And he knew he wasn't the man to give those things to her. He would never be.

He headed for his truck in her driveway, and once inside, replayed Tanya's words. She'd had a tone he'd never heard from her before. It had been sarcastic and mocking and had completely shocked him.

Maybe he hadn't been all wrong to bring Tanya into Lane's sights. It had been obvious by her words and questions that she was extremely jealous of Chelsea. Had that jealousy driven Tanya to want to hurt Chelsea?

As thoughts of Tanya left his mind, visions of Chelsea appeared. He wished he could have shared a slow dance with her tonight. He'd always loved dancing with her. They moved perfectly together to the music, and he had loved the way her body always melded into his own.

She would lean her head into the crook of his neck, and her arms would wind around his neck, and her evocative scent would surround him. He would completely lose himself to the music and to her.

He snapped out of his memories of dancing with Chelsea and pulled away from Tanya's home. Instead of heading back to his ranch, he drove the streets of the small town, hoping to empty his head before going home and going to bed.

His father had loved not only their ranch but also this town where he'd been born and raised like his father before him. Big John had been the person people in Coyote Creek came to for advice, for personal and business loans and support. Johnny hadn't known just how many people in town his father had helped until the murder.

As Johnny leisurely drove down Main Street, he slowed down at each of the stores he knew his father had helped in one way or another. His father had encouraged everyone to shop local and keep their small-town economy strong.

God, he missed his dad. Every day he had a moment of wanting to talk to him, and then he'd remember that he could never talk to him again. The loss would pierce through his heart all over again. His dad would never see him get married or enjoy the grandchildren Johnny would have eventually given him.

It made him so angry that they still had no answers as to who had killed Big John. Dammit, somehow…someway Lane had to solve this murder. Johnny and the rest of his family deserved to know who had done it and why.

Had the murder really been because of a mayoral seat? Or had it had something to do with his father's business dealings? Or, worse than either of those two scenarios, had it been at the hands of his own flesh and blood, a son who had resented his father and had never felt loved by him?

He shoved these dark and troubling thoughts out of his head, knowing he'd never get to sleep tonight if he dwelled on them.

He finally turned down the street where Chelsea lived. He'd been surprised to see how much she'd gotten done the last time he was there. He wasn't surprised that she'd surrounded herself with vivid colors and textures. That's the way he'd always seen Chelsea…as bright colors and different textures and happiness.

As he drew closer to her house, he frowned. Something was in her yard. A sign of some kind. Maybe a poster for her mother's campaign? He'd begun to see them all around town. He pulled closer to the curb, and with the aid of his headlights he saw that it was no kind of campaign sign.

Despite the warmth of the night his blood chilled. The sign read A DEAD WOMAN LIVES HERE… BUT SHE WON'T BE LIVING HERE FOR LONG. THIS DEAD WOMAN WILL BE BURIED SOON. It was a nasty piece of work, obviously meant to terrorize and horrify Chelsea once again.

He could only assume she hadn't seen the sign yet, and as far as he was concerned, she wasn't going to see it. He parked, got out of his truck and strode across the lawn to the sign. He ripped it out of the ground and threw it in the bed of his pickup.

Although he wasn't ready to talk to Chelsea yet, he wanted to make sure she was okay, given the threat of the sign. Her living room light was on and so he crept across the lawn and peeked inside the slightly open blinds.

He breathed a sigh of relief as he saw her sitting on her sofa. She was clad in a nightshirt and was reading a book. She was safe and sound and that's all he cared about. He left the window and strode back to his truck.

Usually on a Friday night Lane was on duty until the bar closed at three, so Johnny drove directly to the police station. Once there, he parked the truck, grabbed the sign and headed inside.

He found Lane leaning over the front desk and chatting with the night receptionist and dispatcher, Walt Eaton. Walt was far beyond retirement years, but nobody knew exactly how old he really was. His hair was completely gray, but his blue eyes snapped with a youthfulness and a keen intelligence.

"Now, that doesn't look like a happy face, Chief, does it?" Walt said. He moved his wheelchair back from the desk. "What's up, Johnny boy?"

Walt had been a deputy and a ranch worker for years. He was a well-known face around the community and had been an especially good friend of Johnny's father. A ranch accident with a tractor had partially paralyzed Walt in his lower limbs, but he was just as feisty as he'd always been.

"Hey, Walt. Lane." Johnny greeted the two and then turned the sign around so the two men could read it.

Walt released a low whistle. "Now, that's some piece of disgusting."

"I'm assuming Chelsea didn't see this, otherwise she'd be here with you," Lane said.

"I'm assuming she didn't see it either. I was on my way home from Tanya's and happened to drive by Chelsea's and found it in her yard. If at all possible, I'd like to keep this just between the three of us," Johnny said. "It's just meant to further terrorize her, and there's really no reason to let her know it was there."

"You know me, Johnny." Walt raised his fingers to his mouth and made a locking motion. "Tick a lock. Nobody will hear anything about this from me."

"Thanks, Walt. I appreciate it." Johnny knew the older man was as good as his word.

"I'm sure as hell not going to tell anyone unless I'm questioning somebody about it. I agree that there's no reason to frighten Chelsea even more than she's already been."

Lane frowned and stared at the sign once again. "It's written all in block letters which is going to make it more difficult to find the author, and I imagine it's written with plain red marker, also nearly impossible to trace."

Lane sighed in obvious frustration. "I've never felt less like a good lawman than in the past month or so. I haven't been able to find your father's killer, and I'm no closer to identifying Chelsea's attacker than the morning she told me about being chased through your pasture."

"Don't beat yourself up too much, Lane. You can only do what's humanly possible in both situations," Johnny said.

"If I find out who killed your daddy, I'll personally get out of this chariot and kick his ass from here to next week," Walt said fervently. "I miss that man, even though he used to beat me so badly in poker I was ashamed to show my face the next day."

A small laugh escaped Johnny. "Thanks, Walt."

"What worries me at the moment is the boldness of leaving this sign," Lane said. "It's announcing that a murder is intended and the potential killer is apparently feeling very confident."

"I'm assuming she got a security system put in?" Johnny asked for confirmation.

"She did. If there's a breach in either her doors or windows, it rings through straight to me and to the dispatcher's desk," Lane replied.

"That should keep her safe as long as she stays in her house," Johnny said with relief. "And I'll be sure to remind her that she needs to stay focused on her surroundings whenever she goes out anywhere."

"Maybe if we're lucky, something will break loose in both cases over the next couple of days," Lane said.

Johnny hoped so. He couldn't really move past his father's death until he had the answers he needed, and he would never be able to live with himself if something horrible happened to Chelsea. But right now that seemed like a very real possibility.

Chapter Eight

Chelsea had no plans to leave her house today. Jeb had called her earlier to tell her he wasn't feeling well and wouldn't be coming in to work. That gave her the perfect excuse to pull on an old pair of jogging shorts and a faded tank top and just chill for the day without seeing anyone.

If she was perfectly honest with herself she would admit that she was licking her wounds after seeing Johnny and Tanya together the night before. It had upset her more than she cared to admit. But she had to get used to it, and she positively had to get over him.

It was strange. She'd just assumed when she returned here Johnny would be lost to her. She'd just figured he'd have moved on, might be married and a family man. However, when she'd come back and found him single, when he'd been so kind to her and when he'd made love to her, she'd truly believed they were destined to be together once again. Now she had to readjust her thinking all over again.

She also had to admit that she'd enjoyed the night out at the Red Barn. As she carried her cup of coffee into her living room and settled in on her sofa, she thought about the night before.

It had been fun to cut loose with Melinda again and see some of the people she'd gone to school with. She'd ended up exchanging numbers with four different guys. They weren't Johnny, but nobody would ever fill the space in her heart that he had.

The standout of the men had been Adam Pearson. She'd ended up dancing with him a couple of times the night before, and if he called to ask her out, she supposed she might go out with him.

Realizing she was sick of thinking about it all, she turned on the television for some mind-numbing entertainment, and for the next hour she merely relaxed and sipped her coffee.

When she'd finished her cup, she paused the television and then headed back into the kitchen for a refill. She had just settled back on the sofa again when her doorbell rang.

Who could it be? Surely none of the men would just casually drop by for a chat so early on a Saturday morning and without calling first.

She jumped back up and approached the front door. Before she looked out the peephole, she ran a hand down her old, comfortable clothes and then through her hair which she'd barely brushed that morning.

She finally looked through the door, and her heart immediately quickened its pace. Johnny. What on earth was he doing here? She turned off the alarm and opened the door. Oh, he looked so handsome in his worn jeans and a blue T-shirt that did absolutely amazing things to his beautiful crystal-blue eyes.

"Hi, Chelsea… Can I come in?"

"Sure." As he moved past her, she caught a whiff of his fresh-scented cologne, and her heartbeat went even faster at the familiar scent. "Uh…would you like a cup of coffee?" she asked.

"That sounds great," he replied. "Do you have time to talk to me?"

"As you can see, I wasn't planning on going anywhere, so I've got all the time in the world. Let me just get your coffee." As he sank down on the sofa she went back into the kitchen.

Jeez, she should have put on better clothes and a little makeup this morning. The last person she'd expected to see this morning was Johnny. Why was he here? She poured a cup for him and then carried it into the living room and set it on the coffee table in front of him.

"Thanks," he said.

She sank down at the opposite end from him and looked at him expectedly. She couldn't begin to guess why he was here or what he might need to talk to her about.

"I was surprised to see you last night at the Red Barn," he said as he picked up the coffee cup.

"Melinda forced me to get out of the house and enjoy a little social time," she replied. "I have to admit I really enjoyed being out and kicking up my heels a little bit."

"I'm glad you enjoyed yourself. You looked really pretty in that red blouse."

"Thank you." A flutter of warmth washed through her at his compliment. "Did you and Tanya have a good time?" she asked even as the thought of the two together hurt her heart.

"It was okay. When we got back to her house, I told her I wouldn't be dating her anymore."

"Oh… Why?" Chelsea's heart renewed its quickened pace. "From what I understood, the two of you had been dating for some time."

"We had been, but I realized last night the relationship wasn't going anywhere and never would. I just saw her as a friend to pass time with, and I thought that it really wasn't fair to her, so I told her we wouldn't be going out together anymore."

"Oh," Chelsea repeated, unsure what to say. She watched him take a sip of the coffee and then place his cup back on the table top. "Uh, how did she take it?"

"Surprisingly badly. I saw a bit of her ugly side when I told her," he replied. "Actually, I was surprised by her unpleasantness."

Chelsea kept her mouth shut tight, even though there was a part of her that wanted to shout *I told you so*. He took another drink, and then an awkward silence ensued.

He finally looked around and then gazed at her with a smile. "The place looks really good, Chelsea." He held the eye contact with her for another long moment and then averted his gaze.

"Thanks." What, exactly, was going on here? Had he just stopped over to compliment her decorating style? Or to tell her he broke up with Tanya? "Johnny, what are you doing here?" she finally asked when the silence had gone on between them for too long.

He leaned back against the sofa and raced a hand through his thick hair and then stared at her intently. "Chelsea, I need some answers."

"Answers? About what?"

"About what happened five years ago. About why I wasn't enough for you. Why didn't I hear about your dreams to become a model in New York before the day you broke up with me and left town? I mean, did I somehow miss something, Chelsea?" His eyes held a shimmer of pain as he held her gaze.

Each word he said broke her heart. She'd never wanted him to think that he had been somehow lacking. Rather, she had been the one who had been lacking in self-worth. She had been the one who had been so broken.

"Oh, Johnny." She moved closer to him on the sofa. "It wasn't about you. It was never about you. It was about me being enough for me. Or, actually, about me not being enough for myself."

She got up, finding it difficult to stay seated and go back to that troubling time in her life. "I shared so many things with you, Johnny." She moved to the other side of the coffee table and began to pace back and forth. "I shared my dreams and my hopes, my passion and love. But there were some things I didn't share with you…things I kept deep inside."

Johnny leaned forward, confusion radiating from his eyes. "Things like what? Tell me, Chelsea. Help me to understand what happened with us."

She stopped moving and forced herself to go back in time. "I was never enough for my mother, and she reminded me of that every day. I know we used to joke about Stella, but you have no idea how much her lack of support or love hurt me, how much it played in my mind. I mean, if my own mother couldn't love me, then how could anyone else?"

"Oh, Chelsea…baby." He started to rise, but she put up her hand to keep him in place. He needed to hear all of it to understand why she had left him.

"Then there was the constant belittling by Tanya and her mean girlfriends. Every day I was told I was ugly and crazy-looking with my big eyes and skinny legs. I was told I looked like an alien or an insect."

She paused, her emotions suddenly threatening to overtake her.

She drew several deep breaths, released them slowly and then continued. "I was also told over and over again that you were dating me out of pity and that the only way I was keeping you was by having wild sex with you. And that was only happening because you probably put a paper bag over my head so you didn't have to look at me."

"Surely you didn't believe any of that," Johnny exclaimed.

She frowned. "When you hear things like that over and over again, it tends to get deep into your head, into your very soul."

"They were bullying you." There was a touch of anger in Johnny's voice. "I knew some of those girls weren't nice to you, but I didn't know the full extent of it. Chelsea, you should have come to me. You should have told me more about it."

"They were pretty careful about not being too mean to me in front of you, but when you weren't around all bets were off. And I didn't tell you because I was embarrassed and ashamed." She began to pace again. "Anyway, on the day I broke up with you, I'd gotten a particularly nasty note telling me how ugly I was and how unworthy I was to be with you. It finally broke me." Tears blurred her vision.

She swiped her cheeks where the hot tears had fallen. "I had to get away from here. I had to get away to figure out who I really was away from the constant noise of Tanya and her friends, away from my critical mother."

Johnny got up and walked over to her. When he reached her, he wrapped his arms around her and gazed intently into her eyes. "You should have told me all this. You should have told me about your insecurities."

She shook her head. "Johnny, don't you understand? You couldn't fix me. No matter how much you told me you loved me, I had to get away and fix myself." She stepped out of his embrace.

"But you must have felt some vindication. You became a top model. People described you as *hauntingly beautiful* and *dramatically gorgeous*." She looked at him in surprise. "I followed your career, Chelsea, and you proved all those mean girls wrong."

"It's funny, I didn't find my self-worth on a runway or through being a model. I found it in the quiet moments I spent alone in my apartment. I spent hours in self-reflection and deciding what was important to me and what was not. I realized it didn't matter what other people thought about my looks. All that was important was how I felt about myself, and I realized I was okay with me."

She turned and walked back to the sofa and flopped down. He quickly joined her there, sitting right at her side. "I wasn't worthy of your love,

Johnny, only because I had to discover my own worth."

"So, what really happened to bring you back here?" he asked.

She knew he was asking about the drug rumors that had plagued her in the tabloids after her infamous fall from a runway. "I'd already decided I wanted to come back here, but I was under contract with my agent, and I intended to finish that out and then move back."

She changed positions as a new rush of emotion swept through her. "It was Fashion Week, and I'd been chosen to walk in a high-profile designer's show. That day when I fell off the runway, I had gotten up that morning not feeling well. I'd been on a four-hundred-calorie-a-day diet for three weeks in order to lose ten more pounds that my agent insisted on, which I needed to do to fit in the dresses I was going to wear. Anyway, I felt a bit light-headed, but knew the show must go on."

Once again a wave of emotion threatened to overwhelm her. She swallowed hard against it. "By the time I got ready to walk the runway, I was dizzy and on the verge of being disoriented, and in the middle of my walk, I passed out and fell. I woke up in the hospital where I was told that I was half-starved and severely dehydrated."

Once again, she took several deep breaths and

let them out slowly. "And that's when the rumors began."

"About you being on drugs," Johnny said softly.

She nodded. "About me doing drugs and having severe mental issues. I have my suspicions about who started those vicious rumors. There was another model. Her model name is Verda. Verda and I seemed to always be pitted against each other when it came to jobs. Usually, I got the jobs over her. I know she hated me, and she was very ambitious, and I believe she started the rumors to get me out. Melinda, as my publicity person, tried her best to fight against the rumors, but in the end nothing she did worked. My agent dropped me, so once I made arrangements to get out of the two apartment leases, I was free to come home."

"Are you going to miss New York?" he asked. "Is there a chance you'll go back to modeling again?"

"No chance whatsoever. My time there was never about the modeling. I know it sounds cliché or like a cop-out, but it was about me finding me, and I did that." She smiled at him. "I don't give a damn if every person in this town thinks I'm ugly. I don't need anyone to define me or try to demean me. I define myself, and I like who I am."

"I'm glad you got what you needed, Chelsea." He hesitated and then asked, "Did you ever think of me while you were gone?"

"Oh, Johnny, I thought about you every night."

She leaned forward and stroked her fingers down the side of his beloved face. "I thought about you all day long, and every night I fell asleep with thoughts of you playing in my mind. But I knew I'd hurt you terribly, and I just figured I'd blown it with you. I expected to come back here and find you married and with a child or two."

"But I saw photos of you out with that actor, and the articles talked about the two of you being madly in love," he said.

She dropped her hand from his face. "Anthony Winchester. The dates were strictly for publicity. Anthony was an arrogant little twit who I found repulsive, but my agent set up the dates in hopes of jump-starting his career. It was always you, Johnny. There has never been anyone else for me."

Her heart trembled in her chest as she held his gaze. She had bared her very soul to him, and there was nothing else she could say.

He frowned and cast his gaze to the wall beside her. When he looked at her once again, his eyes held a sadness that pierced her to her very soul.

In her need to find herself, had she forever lost him? She'd always assumed that had been the price she paid. He'd confirmed that fact after he'd slept with her, but a small hope had ignited in her chest when he'd shown up on her doorstep today. But the sadness she saw on his features doused that optimism.

"I'm just sad that we lost five years together," he finally said.

"I am too," she replied. "When I left here, I never dreamed I'd be away so long. I never dreamed I'd become a model in such demand, and for a while life and time got away from me," she replied.

"Chelsea, it's always been you and only you. I tried like hell to move on from you, but in five years I couldn't."

He leaned toward her. "I want to try it again, Chelsea. Obviously, the timing wasn't right for us before. God help me, but I want to see if we can get it right this time."

He leaned forward and captured her lips in a kiss that shot a sweet warmth through her. It was a kiss that filled her with hope and possibility, even as a small voice whispered inside that it was just possible he might be playing with her heart to get revenge for her breaking his heart years ago.

JOHNNY WALKED OUT of Chelsea's house with the imprint of her lips still warm on his. Even though they had already had sex since she'd been back, they had both agreed to take things slowly this time, and so they were going out to dinner together the next night.

He hadn't known about all the deeply emotional issues she'd been battling years ago, and it somehow hurt that she hadn't been able to share that with him then. He still wasn't sure he trusted a hundred percent that she could be happy here in Coyote Creek. He wasn't totally certain she could be completely happy with him and his quiet ranch life.

There was that little piece of his heart he couldn't quite give to her because he couldn't quite believe she'd be here long-term…to be his forever. And he wanted forever with her.

He was glad he hadn't told her about the sign in her yard, although before he'd left, he'd reminded her that she had to be careful whenever she went out of her house until her would-be attacker was in jail.

When he'd handed the sign over to Lane, before he'd left the police station, the chief had told him he'd checked out both the stalkers Chelsea had mentioned, and both people had been ruled out as suspects. According to the NYPD, one of their officers had checked them out, and both were still in New York and had not traveled recently.

Johnny was therefore back to knowing that her assailant was somebody here in town. Tanya? After having that talk with Tanya on Friday night, he found it much more plausible that it could be her.

While he didn't believe Tanya would really harm anyone, he could see her tormenting Chelsea, especially since she'd shown him a different side of herself the last time he'd spoken to her.

He couldn't believe how truly hateful Tanya and her girlfriends had been to Chelsea all through school. When she'd related to him all the hurtful things they had said to her, his heart had absolutely ached for her.

He had a much better understanding now of the forces that had driven her away from him and from Coyote Creek. And while he wished she had been able to discover her love for herself here in town with him at her side, that simply hadn't been the way it had played out.

Still, his mind returned to the real question at hand. If it wasn't Tanya who was terrorizing Chelsea, then who? Was there some man in town who had harbored a secret rage against Chelsea? Maybe Adam Pearson? Johnny knew Adam as a nice guy, but it had been obvious in the bar that he was interested in Chelsea.

Adam had never married, and as far as Johnny knew he hadn't dated much. Had Adam been obsessed with Chelsea since high school? Had he been angry that he hadn't managed to garner any interest from her?

Johnny mentally shook his head. If he was so good at investigating, he would have solved his father's murder by now. What he really needed to do was get back to the ranch business and leave the investigating to Lane and his force.

Throughout the rest of the afternoon and the next day, all he could think about was having dinner with Chelsea. He realized she wasn't the same rather-fragile young woman who had left Coyote Creek five years ago. She had a new confidence that shone from her eyes, an attitude he found very sexy.

Their relationship would now be different than it had been before. They both had changed and grown over the years apart, and he was eager to explore the changes and see if their relationship was as strong as it had been before the time and distance.

He knew that he was possibly setting himself up for a new heartache where she was concerned. But he'd never be able to truly move on unless he took this one last chance with her. However, he still intended to hold back some pieces of his heart, just in case she took off on him once again.

The next evening when he picked her up for dinner, it was difficult to think about holding back anything. Before he could get out of his pickup, she flew out of her front door with a big smile on her face.

"Hi," she said as she got into his truck.

"Hi, yourself," he replied with a smile of his own. "You look beautiful," he added. She wore a green blouse exactly the color of her eyes and a pair of white capris. White earrings dangled from her ears, and her blond hair sparkled brightly in the sunshine.

"Thanks," she replied. "You clean up real nice too."

He laughed. He hadn't exactly dressed up for dinner at the café. He wore jeans and a button-down, short-sleeved blue shirt. "Thanks. I hope you're hungry."

"I'm absolutely starving. What's the special on Sunday nights?"

"Hot turkey sandwiches with mashed potatoes and gravy and a side of corn casserole and cranberry salad," he replied. As always the scent of her was familiar and enchanting. She smelled like lilacs and sunshine... She smelled like home.

"I'm not sure what I'm going to get, but it's definitely going to include some mashed potatoes," she replied.

"That's good. It wouldn't hurt you to put on some weight." He flashed her a quick glance. "Did I just offend you?"

"No, not at all. I know I'm too thin, and I'm eager to eat my way back to a healthier weight. After starving myself for the last five years, I dream about milkshakes and french fries and chocolate cake and ice cream."

"And here I thought all you ever dreamed about was me," he replied teasingly.

"Oh, yeah, that too." Her eyes sparkled brightly, and then she suddenly frowned. "Are you expecting trouble tonight?"

He knew she was talking about the fact that he had on his holster and gun. "No, not at all. But since my father's murder, I've been wearing my gun most of the time when I go out," he replied, not wanting to worry her about her own situation.

It was true that he'd taken to wearing his gun

whenever he came into town since his father's murder, but now he wore it for a second reason…to protect Chelsea. Nobody was going to harm her as long as she was with him.

Thankfully she didn't press the issue. They had some small talk on the drive to the café. He told her about things on the ranch, and she talked about her quiet day and what she'd watched on television.

Sunday nights the café was always packed, and tonight was no exception. They had to park a block and a half away and walk, but the evening was pleasant, and as he grabbed her hand with his, a swell of deep contentment filled him. The only thing that would have made his life better was if he'd been pushing a stroller with their child in it. But he was getting way ahead of himself.

He didn't quite trust her yet. Despite the conversation they'd shared the day before, he still wasn't a hundred percent sure she was truly here to stay. It was going to take time for him to really be all in with her.

But he wasn't letting any doubts ruin this evening with her. She looked amazing, and despite all the weight that was on his shoulders, a lightness had descended on him the moment Chelsea had climbed into his truck.

They entered the café, and his ears were assaulted by the sounds of happy chatter and laughter and the clink of silverware. The aromas were mouthwatering: warm bread and a variety of meats cooking and sugary treats.

For a moment they stood just inside the door as he looked around for an empty booth or table. He spied an open booth toward the back and led her to it.

They settled in and opened the menus. "Oh my gosh, everything looks so good," Chelsea said.

"Feel free to order whatever your heart desires," he replied.

"What are you having?"

"A steak and a baked potato," he replied without hesitation. "They actually grill a really good steak here."

"I think I'm having the special." She closed the menu. "And chocolate cake for dessert. Does Rosie still own this place?"

"She does." Rosie Graham was a tiny woman who, according to the rumors, ran the café with an iron fist. Even though she had a bit of a temper, she cooked great food and baked like an angel.

"Oh, good. Then I know the cake will be awesome," Chelsea replied.

Their waitress arrived and took their orders, and while they waited for their food they talked about the mild weather that might be broken in the next couple of days with some spring storms in the forecast. He knew she hated storms, but they were a part of living in the Midwest.

They also chatted about who she'd seen at the

Red Door and various people they'd gone to school with. By that time the waitress had arrived with their orders.

For the next few minutes, they were silent as they ate. He loved watching her eat with such gusto. Tanya had always picked at her food and left more on the plate than she ate.

Thoughts of Tanya brought up concerns about the person who was after Chelsea. Was it really possible that jealousy had driven Tanya to attempt the attacks on Chelsea? At least Johnny knew when Chelsea was out with him she was safe, and that's why he'd worn his gun tonight.

They lingered over dessert and coffee. True to her word, she ate a large piece of cake with ice cream and then leaned back against the booth and released a huge satisfied sigh. "I'm totally stuffed," she said.

"Good," he replied. "Ready to take a walk back to my truck?"

She grinned. "I feel like I need to take a four-mile walk to work off some of this food."

"Well, I'm not up for that," he returned with a smile of his own. "A walk to the truck will have to do." He motioned to the waitress to bring the check.

Minutes later they headed to the exit. They nearly bumped into Wayne Bridges and his wife and several other people who were coming in with him.

Johnny immediately stiffened as he eyed the man

who had been running against his father for mayor. Wayne was definitely at the top of the suspect list.

He was a big man with a barrel chest, and hearing him laughing with his friends shot a jagged arrow of grief through Johnny.

If he'd killed Big John and Johnny got evidence of that, he would make sure the man never laughed again.

Chapter Nine

Police chief Lane Caldwell pulled into his driveway, parked and turned off his car. It was just after eleven, and as he got out of his vehicle, a bolt of lightning split the dark skies overhead. A moment later a rumble of thunder sounded.

The wind whipped around him as he hurried to his front door. As he unlocked it, the first raindrops began to fall. The stormy weather definitely was a perfect reflection of his mood.

He stepped into the living room where a lamp in the corner created a soft glow. Despite his mood, he smiled. Rebecca never forgot to turn on the light for him.

As he turned off the lamp, lightning slashed through the darkness followed by a crash of thunder. He walked down the hallway to the master bedroom where Rebecca was sitting up in bed with a book in her lap.

When he saw her a calmness filled him. Her long, brown hair fell around her shoulders and her heart-shaped face was one he never tired of looking at. Unfortunately, they had wanted children but had not been able to have any, but they'd always had each other. When she saw him she put her book on the nightstand next to her.

"I figured you'd be asleep by now," he said to her.

"Really? The storm overhead isn't exactly making lullaby music right now," she replied. She watched as he took off his gun belt and placed it on the top of the chest of drawers. He then sank down on the edge of the bed with a deep sigh.

"You're later tonight than usual for a Wednesday night," she said as he took off his shoes and socks.

"Yeah, I was about ready to come home earlier, but then a call came in from Hannah. Jackson was all liquored up and being combative with her. I headed over there, and it took me about an hour to finally get the man in bed." He stood to finish undressing.

Hannah Elder and her husband, Jackson, were fixtures around town. They were both in their seventies and got along really well until Jackson decided to get his nose in the sauce.

"Just what you need with everything else on your mind."

He nodded as a deep weariness swept over him. He shucked down to his boxers and then went into the adjoining bathroom to wash his face and brush his teeth before bed.

When he was finished, he stared at his reflection in the mirror. He was forty years old, but at the moment he looked like he was closer to fifty.

He frowned and shut off the bathroom light and then returned to the bedroom. He slid into bed, and immediately Rebecca reached for his hand.

"Talk to me, honey," she said softly. After twenty years of marriage, she knew him and all his moods quite well. Tonight, his utter defeat was profound. She squeezed his hand, and her soft blue eyes gazed at him lovingly.

He released a deep sigh. "Maybe it's time I retired."

A small laugh escaped her. "Honey, you're way too young to even think about retiring."

"Then maybe I need to resign and get a job flipping burgers or sweeping floors," he replied.

Once again Rebecca laughed. "You were born to be a law officer. It's the job you always wanted, so what's really going on with you tonight, Lane?"

He released another deep sigh. "I don't know. I'm just feeling more than a bit defeated tonight."

"Are you talking about John King's murder?"

He nodded. "That, and whoever is after Chelsea."

"You can only do what you can do, Lane. You're a good sheriff, a thorough and intelligent man. What exactly happened today that threw you for a loop? What's different today from yesterday?"

"Aside from the fact that I haven't been able to solve these crimes and another day has passed?"

He released her hand and instead raked his hand through his hair. "I got a call from the governor this afternoon. You know he and Big John were good friends. Anyway, the governor wanted to know if I was any closer to finding John's killer, and I had to confess to him that the case has stalled."

"Oh, honey, I know that must have been difficult for you." Rain began to pelt against the window as the storm continued to rage. It seemed somehow appropriate that they would be talking about murder and mayhem on a dark and stormy night. "I know Johnny mentioned that he wanted you to look at Caleb for the crime. Have you interviewed him again?"

"I have. He told me when the murder occurred, he was in a field taking pictures of things he wanted to paint."

"Do you believe him?"

"I do. He's a strange man. Maybe I'm missing something, but I just can't see him killing his own father. I feel it in my gut that Wayne is behind the murder. Unfortunately, my gut instinct isn't enough to bring him in for an arrest."

Rebecca straightened up. "Do you really think Wayne actually pulled the trigger?"

Lane had thought about that question for some time now. "I don't think Wayne would actually get his hands dirty. He's got a couple of ranch hands who are fiercely loyal to him. One of them, Peter Jeffries, has won a number of marksmanship medals. He's a deadeye with a rifle. I think he's the one who actually pulled the trigger, and I think he was probably paid a handsome price for doing it. But so far there's no sign of any money exchanged between the two."

"If Wayne or one of his minions really killed John because John was set to become the next mayor, then you better warn Stella Black, because right now it looks like she's beating the pants off the competition," Rebecca said.

"I already spoke to her about it. I told her she needed to watch her back, and since then I've noticed that when she's out and about town, she has a couple of her ranch hands with her as obvious protection."

"As far as John's murder, I believe sooner or later somebody is going to get drunk and say too much, and the killer will be exposed."

"That would be nice," Lane replied.

"As far as Chelsea is concerned, sooner or later the perp will overplay his hand, and he'll be exposed as well."

"Aren't you the optimist tonight?" Lane said with a weary smile at her.

"I just believe good will always overcome evil. I also know that secrets are hard to keep in this town. Eventually you'll get the bad guys in jail. I have complete faith in you, Lane."

He leaned forward and kissed the woman who

had been and still was his lover, his partner and his best friend. "I love you, my sweet Becky."

She placed her hand on his cheek, her gaze soft. "And I love you, my sweet Lane." She dropped her hand from his face, "Now, what you need to do is get some sleep. You've been working long hours, and I know how exhausted you've been."

"I am tired," he admitted.

"It sounds like the storm is passing, and hopefully you'll have good dreams and deep rest," she replied. "Ready for the light to go out?"

"Ready."

A half an hour later Lane remained wide awake, a million thoughts chasing sleep away. The governor's call to him today had added immeasurable pressure on him. He had no idea if Johnny was behind the call or not. It didn't really matter.

The call was a reminder of just how powerful the King family was, and if they decided to use that power against Lane, they could oust him from office.

Still, Rebecca was right. He could only do what he could do, and right now the odds were stacked against him. He had a murderer running loose in his town, and another would-be killer plotting against Chelsea.

How soon before the person plotting against Chelsea made another move? How soon before that person was successful in killing her?

How long before John's murderer decided somebody else needed to die? How emboldened would he be, given he'd already gotten away with killing somebody?

Lane finally fell asleep and into dreams of faceless shooters and ski-masked monsters.

CHELSEA GOT OUT of her car and nervously ran her hand down her navy skirt. She hoped the navy-and-white blouse coupled with the skirt she had on gave her a professional look. For the first time in a long time, she was going to apply for a real job.

It didn't matter that she was applying for a job in Johnny's sister's store. She was still nervous about it. In the past week she'd given a lot of thought as to what she wanted to do with her life.

She knew working in Ashley's store would be fun. The store contained a variety of beautiful knick-knacks and candles, lovely costume jewelry and a small rack of colorful dresses. It was the kind of place she'd love to work.

She hadn't told Johnny she was applying for a job with his sister. She didn't want him to put in a good word for her, and she definitely didn't want Ashley to feel any pressure to hire her.

Smoothing her skirt one last time, Chelsea walked into the store. A tiny bell tinkled to announce her arrival. The air inside smelled pleasantly of fresh spring flowers and ocean waters.

"Hi, Chelsea," Ashley greeted her from a chair

behind the glass counter that displayed the jewelry and held a cash register on top.

"Hi, Ashley," Chelsea replied.

Ashley moved from behind the counter, a smile on her lips as she approached where Chelsea stood just inside the door. "Is there anything specific you're looking for today that I can help you with?"

"A job?"

Ashley looked at her in surprise. "Are you serious?"

"Dead serious. I'd love to work here, Ashley. I love what you sell, and I could seriously sell all the items with enthusiasm to shoppers." Chelsea shut her mouth, aware that maybe she was coming on too strong.

"Why don't you come on back to my office where we can sit and chat." Ashley led the way to the back of the store and through a beaded curtain.

Ashley's so-called office consisted of two folding chairs set up amid boxes of inventory. Ashley sat on one and gestured Chelsea to the other.

"Ashley, I certainly don't want you to feel any pressure about this just because I'm back together with Johnny," Chelsea said hurriedly.

"Thanks, Chelsea. I appreciate that." Ashley frowned thoughtfully. "Actually, you approaching me about this now is perfect timing. It's been just me running this shop since I opened it, but I've been working twelve-hour days, and I don't have time for anything else. Since Dad's death I really need to spend more time with my mom, and I've been considering hiring somebody here to help me out."

"Ashley, I'd be available to work whatever hours you need me to," Chelsea replied.

"Okay, then. You're hired."

"I am?" A wave of excitement swept through Chelsea. "That was way easier than I expected."

Ashley laughed. "You just happen to be the right person who showed up at the right time."

"I promise you won't regret hiring me. I'm reliable, and I'll work hard for you."

Her new boss smiled. "Why don't you come in tomorrow morning about nine, and I'll train you on the register, then we can talk about your hours."

Chelsea jumped up from the chair. "Thanks, Ashley. I'll see you at nine tomorrow."

Ashley got up, and together the two women headed back toward the front door. "By the way, how are things going with you and Johnny?" Ashley asked.

"Good. We're still taking things slow and learning how we've each changed in the last five years," Chelsea replied.

Ashley held her gaze for a long moment. "Just don't break his heart again, Chelsea."

"I'm all in with him, Ashley. I love him with all my heart. I've always loved him, and I'm hoping he will be my happily-ever-after."

Ashley held her gaze for another long moment and then nodded as if satisfied by what she saw. "I'm hoping that too."

"Thanks. I'll see you in the morning." Chelsea walked out to cloudy skies, but she felt as if the sun was shining in her heart.

Things were going well with Johnny, and she had landed a job she was looking forward to performing. When she got into the car, her first thought was to call Johnny and tell him about her new job, but she decided to wait. He was coming over for dinner, and she'd tell him then.

The past week she'd seen Johnny twice, although they had talked on the phone every evening before bedtime. She would have loved to be in his bed each night, but he had been serious about taking things slowly.

There had been no more lovemaking between them. Instead they spent their time together talking about both silly and serious topics. They were learning things about each other…things that had changed about themselves during the time they had been apart.

Nothing she'd learned about Johnny had changed her mind about him. He was still the man she loved… would always love. She wanted to marry him and be his wife. She wanted to give him babies and build a family with him.

But Johnny hadn't offered to give her engagement

ring back. She sensed that he was holding back, and that scared her more than a little bit. She'd told Ashley the truth: she was all in with Johnny. She always had been, despite the difficult choice she'd made years ago.

She just wasn't sure if he was all in on her. She couldn't blame him for being a bit wary, given what she'd done to him years ago. All she could do was keep on telling him that he was the one and only for her and that she would love him through eternity. Hopefully he'd quickly come to believe that she was his forever.

She arrived at her house, which was now newly painted an attractive light gray with darker gray shutters at all the windows. She immediately headed for the kitchen.

Tonight, she was showing Johnny her love for him by cooking one of his favorite meals. She knew he loved his mother's spaghetti and meatball recipe, so the day before she'd called Margaret to get the recipe.

Right now, she needed to get the tomato sauce cooking and then add the meatballs in to cook with the sauce. Thankfully it was relatively early so she'd have it all ready by six o'clock when Johnny was set to arrive.

Forty-five minutes later she dropped the last meatball into the simmering sauce. She then made herself a cup of coffee and sank down at the table.

Her gaze automatically went to the back door, where the plywood still covered the broken windowpanes. She should have had the door fixed by now, but for some reason she'd been reluctant to do so. The plywood was a reminder she needed to be careful when she was out and about and when she was home alone.

Thankfully, nothing frightening had happened since that night. She hoped that whoever hated her was over it now and any threat against her was gone. Still, she intended to remain vigilant. Certainly, the alarm system made her sleep more easily at night and feel safe whenever she was in the house.

She jumped as her phone rang. She picked it up to see that the caller identification said *A. Pearson.* "Hi, Adam," she said when she answered.

"Hey, Chelsea. How are things going with you?" His voice was deep and friendly.

"Good. What about you?"

"Life has been good. I'm staying busy at my office. You know I sell insurance…have my own agency now."

"No, I didn't know that. Congratulations on having your own agency," she replied.

"Thanks. Anyway, life has been going good, but it would be much better if you would go out with me this Friday night. Maybe have some dinner at the café and then kick up our heels at the Red Barn." He laughed. "I'm calling because I finally got up the nerve to ask you out."

"Oh, Adam. I'm so sorry, but Johnny and I are back together."

There was a moment of silence, and then he laughed again. "Wow, that certainly happened fast. I guess that means I'm out in the cold once again." His voice sounded less friendly now.

"What do you mean by *out in the cold once again*?" she asked curiously.

"All through high school I kept waiting for a blip in your relationship with Johnny so I could get a chance to go out with you."

"Really," she replied in stunned surprise.

"Yeah. I told you the other night at the Red Barn that I had a major crush on you back then. I meant what I said. Oh, well, I guess Johnny wins again."

"I'm so sorry, Adam. I hope you find the woman who is perfect for you."

"Yeah, thanks. I'll see you around." He didn't wait for her reply before hanging up.

Chelsea set her cell phone back on the table. She'd definitely found the brief conversation a bit troubling. Was it possible Adam had resented her all through high school? Was it possible his resentment had grown through the years and he hated her so much now he'd come after her? It sounded crazy, but murders had happened for lesser motives.

Was Adam her stalker? A shiver suddenly walked up her spine. If so, had she just given him another reason to hate her…to want to kill her?

JOHNNY PULLED UP in front of Chelsea's house, and a sweet rush of anticipation swept through him. It had been a couple days since he'd seen her. The storms that had blown through a couple of days ago had partially ripped down a tin-roofed outbuilding, and since that time he and two of his ranch hands had been working late into the evenings to fix the building.

If he followed his heart, he would tell her to sell her house and move in with him. But his head still wasn't all in with her. He still had doubts about her being happy here after the glamorous way she'd lived in New York City. He just wished he could convince himself she was truly here to stay. He didn't even know for sure what would have to happen for him to give her the last pieces of his heart.

He was adamant that they take things slowly. While he would have gladly taken her to bed and made love to her night after night, he wanted to keep their sexual relationship out of it for now. It was easy to love Chelsea when they were making love, but he wanted to make sure their relationship was much deeper than the physical pull they had toward each other.

He got out of the truck and a moment later knocked on the door. She answered with a wide smile that instantly warmed his heart. "Come on in," she said invitingly.

"Hmm, something smells really good," he said as he stepped inside.

"It's one of your favorites. Spaghetti and meatballs. I even called your mother yesterday to get the recipe."

"You did?" He grinned at her. "Mom actually gave you her secret recipe?"

"She did, and I followed it to a T. Come sit down. Let's chat a bit before we eat," she said.

He sat on the sofa next to her. As always, she looked beautiful clad in a pair of jeans and a green-and-white-striped blouse. Her green eyes sparkled brightly as she faced him. "Guess what."

"What?" he replied.

"I got a job today."

He looked at her in surprise. "Really? Where?"

"I start tomorrow morning at your sister's shop."

"How did that come about?" He was happy she had gotten a job. He didn't think it was healthy for anyone to sit around day after day with nothing to do. He believed it was important that people worked, no matter what kind of work it was. It promoted a sense of pride and confidence.

"I went in to talk to her this morning and walked out with the job." She looked at him proudly. "And I don't think it had anything to do with the fact that you and I are back together."

"That's great, Chelsea, and Ashley wouldn't have

hired you if she didn't think you'd be an asset, family ties be damned."

Her smile grew thoughtful. "I'm also kind of thinking about starting a blog."

"A blog about what?" he asked curiously. He didn't know that much about social media things other than online banking and paying bills.

"I was thinking about it being a kind of cautionary tale about the modeling world. Letting young girls know that compromising their health isn't an option and things like that. I'd like to educate young women on what is acceptable and what is not."

Once again, he looked at her in surprise. "I think that would be a great thing for you to do."

"I'll probably get some haters, but I'm prepared for that," she continued.

He reached out and took one of her hands in his. "Well, you can believe that I'm going to be one of your biggest fans."

She smiled and squeezed his hand then released it. "Then let's move into the kitchen, and I'll feed my biggest fan."

Minutes later they were at the table. She'd not only made the spaghetti and meatballs but also a salad and garlic bread. As they ate she continued to talk about her excitement about starting the job with Ashley and the blog. He then told her about the wind damage that had taken down some branches and the tin on the outbuilding.

"You may have some more wind damage to contend with before this week is over," she said. "There are more storms in the forecast."

"Yeah, that's what I've heard. This is working up to be one of the stormiest springs that I can remember," he replied.

"You'll want all this rain back about July or August when everything is dry and burning up."

He laughed. "You're right about that."

"Still, I'm not looking forward to more storms." She shivered. "Thunder still makes me afraid." She laughed then. "I guess I'm just a big baby."

"You're my baby," he replied, winning one of the smiles from her that made him believe everything was right in the world.

"You know, back to speaking about jobs, the biggest job I'm most looking forward to is that of being a mom," she said.

"Are you still thinking two children…a boy and a girl?" he asked.

"That's always what our plan was."

"Well, my plan has changed," he said.

Instantly a sliver of apprehension danced into her eyes. "Changed how?" she asked.

"I'm thinking I'd like to have two boys and two girls."

She laughed. "And why don't we throw in a set of triplets while we're at it?"

"Works for me," he replied with a grin.

They remained at the table after eating, laughing about some of the more ridiculous plans they had made when they'd been young and in love, including living in a tent if they couldn't afford a house.

The mood remained light and fun until they were cleaning up the dishes and she told him about her conversation with Adam Pearson.

When she finished, his stomach was tied in a knot as he considered what she'd told him. Adam Pearson? Was it possible he was her perp? Had he secretly harbored a resentment toward her that had exploded out of control when she'd come back to town?

Adam had never married and only rarely dated. Was that because he'd had some sort of an obsessive love for Chelsea? While the man had always been affable to Johnny, who knew what dark secrets he might hold in his mind? And was one of those secrets his obsessive love turned to abject hatred of Chelsea?

If Johnny found out Adam was behind the terrorizing of Chelsea, he would give him a beatdown that the man would never forget. Then he would turn him over to Lane to make sure he was prosecuted to the fullest extent of the law.

Chapter Ten

At promptly nine o'clock the next morning, Chelsea walked into Ashley's shop, Bling and Things. There was a display table when customers first walked in showcasing new items that had arrived in the shop. Once past the display table, the store was divided into four long aisles of fare for sale. Across the back of the store was a rack for clothing and accessories.

Ashley greeted her with a big smile. Today Chelsea's new boss looked particularly pretty with her long black hair pulled into a high, stylish ponytail that showed off her high cheekbones and bright blue eyes.

"There's nothing I love more than people who show up on time," she said.

"I've always believed it's the height of rudeness to be late and make somebody else wait," Chelsea replied.

"You're speaking my language now," Ashley replied with a laugh.

For the next two hours she taught Chelsea how to

work the register, how the inventory was stored and then told her to wander around the store and familiarize herself with all the items for sale.

Chelsea wandered the aisles and racks and took notes about the various things, not only for selling but also making a separate list of things she'd like to buy for herself.

It was about noon when Ashley handed her a schedule of her work days and hours. Chelsea was pleased to see it was a mix of morning and evening hours, although she had a feeling Johnny was going to give her a hard time about the evening hours as long as her stalker was still on the loose.

But she was being careful. Every time she went outside, she checked her surroundings to make sure nobody was lurking nearby. She carried pepper spray in her purse, and she now thought it was possible that Adam was the person who had chased her through the field and tried to break into her house, so she was definitely keeping an eye out for him.

While Chelsea was still in the shop, two women came in, and Ashley asked Chelsea to take care of them. One of the women wandered around the store and then left without making a purchase. The second woman bought a lovely silver vase, and Chelsea successfully rang up the sale.

When the woman left, the shop was quiet. "Ashley, are you dating anyone?" Chelsea asked curiously.

"Nobody in particular. I'm still waiting for my knight in shining armor," she replied.

"In this town you're more likely to find a dusty cowboy wearing jeans," Chelsea said with a laugh.

"That's okay. I'm looking for a man like my brothers. Johnny and Luke are good men with fairly fierce facades and gentle souls. They have good values and morals, and that's what I want in a man."

"You don't have to explain to me why you'd want to find somebody like them. I don't know about Luke, but I know Johnny is my knight in shining armor. He always has been and always will be."

"Johnny told me about the issues you've been having. Aren't you terrified?"

"Not so much now that I have a home security system installed."

"But what about when you aren't at home?" Ashley's blue eyes were wide.

"I'm being careful and watching my surroundings. Besides, I'm not going to live my life like a hermit and never leave my house just because some creep is after me."

"Do you have any idea who is after you?" Ashley's eyes grew even wider.

Chelsea thought about mentioning Adam but then decided not to. She wasn't sure he was her boogeyman, and it wouldn't be prudent to throw his name out there without any real evidence against him. "I have some suspicions, but I really don't know who it is for sure."

"Have you considered that it might be Tanya? I know she was really hateful to you in the past, and she was really into Johnny. He dropped her pretty fast after he learned you were back in town."

"That might be, but I considered her, and I just can't see her taking any jealousy issues she might have with me this far. I can't see her chasing me across a pasture or swinging a scythe."

Ashley narrowed her gaze. "I wouldn't put anything past that woman. I couldn't stand her when Johnny was dating her. She was dismissive and rude to me when he wasn't around."

Chelsea laughed. "Welcome to my world."

"I tried to tell him how nasty she was, but he thought I was being overly sensitive." Ashley reached out and took one of Chelsea's hands in hers. "I'm so glad you're back, Chelsea, and I'm so happy you and Johnny have found your way back together again. You've always been family."

"Stop it, or you're going to make me cry," Chelsea said with a strangled laugh.

Ashley laughed and released her hand. "That's the last thing I want."

"Still, I really appreciate the sentiment, Ashley. I've always felt like part of your family. Even while I was away I wanted to be back in your home with your mom fussing in the kitchen and your dad doling out words of wisdom from his armchair." Chelsea's heart clutched at thoughts of Big John. "Oh, Ashley, I can't imagine how much you must miss him."

"I was his princess, and he was my hero," Ashley said, her blue eyes misting with the threat of tears. "It just happened so fast. One minute he was here, and the next minute he was gone, but now I'm particularly worried about both Johnny and Luke."

"Why?" Chelsea asked in surprise. "I mean, I know they are grieving, but that's only natural."

"I worry about Johnny because he is trying to be the be-all and end-all for everyone. He's not only carrying the weight of the ranch business but also trying to hold the family together. Luke worries me even more."

"How so?"

Ashley frowned. "I've never seen him as intense as he is right now. He's so angry about Dad's murder, and he's not healing in any way. I'm worried that in his absolute need to find out who killed Dad, he's going to do something stupid and get himself in trouble."

"Have you talked to Johnny about him?" Chelsea asked.

Ashley shook her head. "No, because I don't want to add to Johnny's burdens right now. I'm just hoping that with more time, Luke will calm down and not go chasing after trouble."

"I'm sure Lane is doing everything he can to find the murderer."

"I'm sure he is too. I just wish there were more clues or some evidence pointing to the guilty person."

Their conversation was halted by two women coming into the shop. "You're good to go for today, Chelsea," Ashley said. "Just be careful when you're out and about."

As Ashley greeted the customers, Chelsea slid out of the door.

Dark clouds had rolled in overhead, usurping the sunshine with a semidarkness. True to what she and Johnny had talked about the night before, the forecast was for a stormy afternoon and an even stormier night.

She'd always had a bit of fear where storms were concerned. She'd been afraid of the thunder and lightning since she was a little girl with nobody to soothe or calm her fears.

She had only run to her mother's bed once in fear of a storm, and Stella had told her to stop being a big baby and had sent her back to her room. Chelsea had been about five years old at the time. She had never sought comfort from her mother again.

At least it hadn't started to rain yet, she thought as she hurried to her car. She had no plans to see Johnny tonight. He was setting the pace in this new relationship, but it was way too slow as far as she was concerned.

However, she refused to push him where their relationship was concerned, especially after talking with Ashley. She'd never want to be an additional burden on Johnny. She wanted to be his support, his quiet and soft place to fall.

She still couldn't believe she was getting a second chance with him, that after so many years apart they had found each other again. She wasn't about to blow it up by rushing him in any way. Still, she longed to have her engagement ring back on her finger and to have that ultimate commitment from him.

Heck, she didn't even know if he still had the beautiful diamond ring he had given to her before. For all she knew he'd sold it or lost it or thrown it in the trash after she had given it back to him. She wouldn't have blamed him if he'd gotten rid of it.

At least it would be a perfect afternoon and evening to play around with the idea of a blog. She could lock the doors, put on some jammin' music and play around with a ring light and the blogging equipment she'd received in the mail the day before.

It was going to be a stormy night, but she'd be safe and sound and enjoying the evening all by herself.

"I'M THINKING ABOUT adding a horse-breeding business," Johnny said to Luke. The two men were seated in Johnny's living room. A preternatural darkness had fallen with the thickening of storm clouds. Even though it was only six thirty in the evening, Johnny had turned on the lamps on either side of the sofa to battle the encroaching darkness.

"What?" Luke asked. It was obvious he had been distracted since he'd come to Johnny's cabin after dinner.

Johnny repeated himself and then added, "And I'm hoping you'll take the helm of this new endeavor. What do you think about it?"

Luke frowned thoughtfully. "I know Dad had talked about starting a horse-breeding program before he…before he died…before he was murdered. I guess I might be up for something like that."

"Great. I've done some research, and I'll email what I have to you, but there's a lot more research that needs to be done. Once you have a plan together, we'll sit down with Mom and Caleb and Ashley and take a family vote on moving forward with the new project."

"Caleb sure as hell won't care what we do with the ranch as long as he gets enough allowance to buy new canvas and paint and booze," Luke replied. "And Ashley completely trusts us when it comes to the ranch business."

"True, but we've always made decisions as a family," Johnny said. "We need to get their approval for spending money on purebred horses, and we'll need to add on to the stables, among a bunch of other things."

Luke got up from the sofa and began to pace in front of Johnny's recliner. "You do realize the more time that passes, the less of a chance Lane is going to find the murderer. It's basically become a cold case."

Johnny released a small sigh. He'd hoped by giving Luke the horse program it would give him something else to think about. Luke was being eaten alive by his grief and rage, and Johnny didn't know how to help him.

"Luke, we might never know who killed him," Johnny finally said.

Luke's gaze burned into Johnny's. "I can't accept that. I can't live like that. Somebody has got to pay for this."

"Luke, we all miss him, and I want somebody arrested for the murder as much as you do. But you can't let this eat you up. You need to figure out how to let go of some of your anger and move on."

"I'll let it go when Lane arrests somebody for the crime. In the meantime, I intend to do a little sleuthing on my own. I really believe Wayne Bridges is behind it, and I think one of his ranch hands actually pulled the trigger. I'm not sure which one did it, but I'm going to find out."

Johnny got out of his chair, and at the same time a rumble of thunder sounded in the distance. "Luke, don't do anything foolish. I need you here on the ranch and not in a jail cell for harassing somebody."

"Don't worry about me, Johnny. I can do some investigating without harassing anyone. I'm not about to get arrested for trying to find my father's killer." It thundered once again as if to punctuate his words.

"I'd better get to my place before it really starts storming," Luke added and headed for the front door.

Johnny walked with him, and as Luke opened the door, Johnny grabbed him by the arm. "Luke, you've got to let some of this go and get back to living your life. I need your time and energy focused on this horse program."

"I hear you," Luke replied and pulled away from Johnny. "Don't worry about me, brother."

"I care about you, and it hurts me to see you in so much pain."

Luke reached out and patted his older sibling on the shoulder. "I love you too, bro. Send me the stuff you have about breeding programs, and I'll do more research and get back to you with a plan for going forward."

With that, Luke stepped outside and headed to his own place. Johnny watched him go and then returned to his chair, and when he sat down a deep sigh escaped him.

Over the last week, he'd seen Luke wind himself tighter and tighter. Johnny had always planned on expanding the business by getting into horse breeding, but he'd intended to do it sometime in the future.

He'd changed his mind and decided to explore it right now hoping it would be a distraction for Luke from his all-consuming grief. However, Luke wasn't the only person Johnny was concerned about. Caleb was drinking and, Johnny suspected, drugging more than ever before.

Johnny didn't believe Leroy Hicks was a good influence on his youngest brother, and he still had the feeling that somehow the two were up to no good.

Johnny had tried several times in the last week to engage with Caleb. He'd asked if he could see some of Caleb's paintings, but Caleb had told him no.

"I'm preparing for a sidewalk sale," Caleb had said. "And I don't want anyone to see my work right now. It will all be on display very soon. Besides, nobody in this family has ever been interested in what I was doing before."

"Who is sponsoring this sidewalk sale?" Johnny had asked.

"Nobody. I'm setting it up on the empty lot between the feed store and the post office."

"Don't you need a permit or something like that?"

Caleb had smiled slyly. "I'm a King. Nobody would dare shut me down. I don't need some stupid permit."

All Johnny could hope for was that Caleb would be successful and sell lots of paintings. It would certainly be good for his self-esteem, and maybe it would help him really turn his life around.

As the thunder boomed overhead, Johnny picked up his cell phone and called Chelsea. She answered on the first ring. "Hi, Johnny."

Just the sound of her voice lightened his mood more than a little bit. "What are you doing?"

"I've been playing around with this blog idea. For the last hour I've been trying to take a decent selfie to put on a web page. I've always had people photograph me. I never learned the fine art of a selfie."

"It can't be that hard. Just point the camera at your face and click a picture," he replied.

"In the point-and-clicks I've taken so far, my nose looks too big or my ears look like Dumbo's. My smiles make me look either like a madwoman who escaped from an asylum or so vacuous it's pathetic. I know everyone is supposed to have a good side, but so far I can't find mine on either side."

He laughed. "Baby, I'm sure in every photo you take you're absolutely beautiful."

"Spoken like a truly good boyfriend," she replied.

"Sounds like you're being too hard on yourself."

"Maybe," she replied dubiously.

Once again thunder rumbled. "It's going to be stormy tonight," he said.

"I know, but I'll be all right. I'm a big girl now, and maybe if the lightning illuminates my bedroom just right, I'll manage to get a good selfie."

Once again, he laughed, pleased that she sounded so strong and so charming at the same time. "I hope that happens for you. Maybe tomorrow we can go out to dinner at the café and you can show me your perfect selfie shot."

"That sounds like a plan," she replied. "If I manage to get a good one by then."

"I'll pick you up around six o'clock. Does that work for you?"

"Yeah. Tomorrow morning I'm working from nine until two, so I've got my evening free."

"Chelsea, I love that you're taking steps to have a good life here," he replied. Each step she took gave him more and more confidence that she wasn't going to take off and run from Coyote Creek again.

"That's my goal. I want a great life here with you, Johnny. I don't want to depend on you. I like that I have a job and that I'm building a bit of a life separate from you. I think it's important for me to have something just for myself. I think it's healthy for both of us."

He smiled into the phone. "I agree."

"I don't just want to be Johnny's girlfriend or Johnny's wife. I need to have an identity that's all my own. You're Johnny King, the cattle baron, and now I'll be Chelsea, that girl who works in Ashley's shop."

He laughed once again. "Ah, Chelsea. I knew you would cheer me up."

"Did you need cheering up?" she asked with obvious concern in her tone. "What's going on, Johnny?"

"Oh, it's nothing. I'm just a little bit concerned about Luke," he admitted.

"Ashley mentioned the same thing when I saw her this morning," Chelsea said.

For the next few minutes Johnny talked about his worries about both of his brothers.

"Johnny, you can't take on the burdens of the world. You can't heal them. That's something only they can do for themselves."

"Thanks, Chelsea. I guess I needed to hear that." They spoke for a few more minutes, and then he finally bade Chelsea good-night. The minute he hung up the phone he looked forward to talking to her again, to seeing her.

He knew she was just waiting for him to ask her to marry him again. He got up out of his chair and walked into his office. Built into the wall next to his desk was a safe. He crouched in front of it and spun the combination lock and then opened it.

Inside was important paperwork for the plot of land where his cabin was located, deeded to him by his father and mother, among other things. Far in the back, beneath all the papers, was a small velvet box.

He pulled it out and opened it, exposing the two-and-a-half-carat diamond in an elaborate gold setting. At the time he'd given Chelsea the ring, he'd believed they would be together always. The day she had given the ring back to him had been one of the worst days in his life.

Was he ready to give her the ring back? Was he ready to reinvest with his whole heart and soul into the dreams they had once shared? That they might share again?

He just wasn't sure.

Chapter Eleven

It was almost nine o'clock, and the full brunt of the storm had just begun to rage overhead. The wind whipped the tree outside her bedroom window, making the branches tap...tap...tap on the glass. Amid the taps of the tree, rain slashed down.

Lightning slashed the skies, and thunder boomed overhead. Chelsea tried to ignore the storm even as her heartbeat raced a little faster.

She told herself nothing happening outside could hurt her. Instead of focusing on the storm, she continued to research how to build a web site and blog.

One thing she had definitely learned over the last few hours: building a professional-looking web page was way beyond her pay grade. She'd spent the last hour researching people who built them for a living.

She finally settled on two people who looked interesting and wrote down their names and contact information. She intended to contact them both first thing in the morning about building her web site.

She wanted to see what each of them would bring

to the table, then she could make her final decision as to who would work for her. And if those two didn't work out, then she could do some more research. At least she'd finally managed to get a decent selfie.

The night was now complete. She'd spoken to Johnny, and she'd worked hard, and now she was hoping that the storm would pass quickly so she could get a good night's sleep.

She changed into a black nightshirt that had stars and the moon across the front and then stood in front of her closet to pick out her clothes for the next morning.

She knew it was important for her to look professional for working in the shop. She wanted to look classy, yet trendy, to reflect the ambience of the place. She finally pulled out a pair of white slacks with a red-and-white tri-cut blouse and bold red earrings.

A loud banging came from someplace downstairs. Her heart leaped into her throat. What was it? Had a shutter come loose in the wind? Was somebody trying to get in? The alarm hadn't gone off.

She walked halfway down the stairs and realized the banging was somebody at her front door. Who on earth would be here at this time of night and in the middle of a storm?

She hurried to the door and peered outside. With a gasp of surprise, she quickly unarmed the alarm and unlocked and opened the door. "Melinda, what on earth are you doing here?" She grabbed her friend's arm and yanked her through the door. Melinda's oversize purse smacked into the wall as she reeled inside. Chelsea locked the door and set the alarm, then turned back to Melinda.

"Oh my gosh, you're soaking wet. Wait there and let me go get you a towel." Chelsea quickly ran into the guest bathroom just off the living room and grabbed a thick fluffy towel, then hurried back to Melinda whose dark hair had curled up to make her look like a bedraggled poodle.

"Thanks." Melinda took the towel from her and dried her hair and then ran the towel down her shoulders. She then handed the towel back to Chelsea, who returned it to the bathroom.

By that time Melinda had parked herself on the sofa. "What are you doing here at this time of night in this kind of weather?" Chelsea asked as she sank down next to her friend.

"I couldn't wait until morning to tell you." Melinda's brown eyes sparkled brightly.

"To tell me what?" Chelsea asked.

"To tell you this." She thrust her hand out, exposing a diamond ring. "I'm engaged," she squealed.

Chelsea squealed back, and the two hugged each other. "Wait. This calls for a champagne toast," Chelsea said. "I'll be right back."

Chelsea ran into the kitchen to the cabinet that

held her liquor. She tried to always keep champagne for any special occasions that might come along. And this was definitely one of them.

She carried the bottle and two crystal stemmed glasses back into the living room. "Ta-da," she said as she managed to open the bottle with a pop but no spray. She poured the two glasses and handed one to Melinda.

"To you and Roger and love forever more," she said.

"I'll drink to that," Melinda said with a girlish giggle.

The two clinked their glasses together, sipped the drink and then Chelsea set her glass on the coffee table. "Now, tell me all about it. How did Roger ask you?" Chelsea asked.

Lightning flashed outside the window, and the thunder boomed loudly. "It was so sweet," Melinda said. "We had dinner at the café like we usually do when we go out. Normally Roger is pretty laid back when we eat out. But tonight, he ate fast and encouraged me to eat quickly as well. I thought maybe he was eager to get rid of me."

"Did you tell him that you were upset?"

"When we were finished with our meals, I told him how I was feeling, that I felt like he was rushing the time with me, and it was hurting my feelings. He immediately apologized and said we'd linger over coffee and dessert. So, I ordered my usual, a piece of strawberry cream cake, and when it came the ring was on the top of it. Suddenly Robert fell to one knee right there in the café, and he asked me to marry him. When I said yes, everyone in the place stood up and cheered."

"Oh my gosh, how exciting! You must be thrilled. Girl, I'm so very happy for you," Chelsea said and leaned over to hug Melinda once again. "Have you set a date yet?" She straightened up again.

"Yeah, September 15."

"This September?" Chelsea asked in surprise. "That doesn't give you much time."

Melinda nodded. "It's just going to be a small affair. Roger doesn't want a huge ceremony that costs us a fortune. He'd much rather we save the money so we can buy a house, and I agree with him."

"Still, you want a nice ceremony. Hopefully it will be the only wedding you get, and you and Roger will live happily ever after."

Melinda laughed. "Trust me, I only intend to have this one wedding and stay happily married forever. Now, I have a question to ask you. I'd like you to be my only bridesmaid."

Chelsea's heart swelled with happiness. "Oh, Melinda, I'd be honored to be your bridesmaid."

"You know we swore we'd be in each other's weddings when we were about fourteen years old," Melinda reminded her.

"And we elaborately planned our weddings before we were old enough to even know how to kiss a boy. Have you thought about what colors you want?"

For the next thirty minutes or so, as the storm continued to rage overhead, the two talked about the wedding. Chelsea was thrilled for her friend, but she couldn't help but wish she was also planning her own wedding.

Still, it was fun to talk about Melinda's special day. They talked about dresses and food, flowers and music. They laughed together as the ideas grew more outrageous and over-the-top.

Finally, Melinda stood. "I've taken up enough of your time. I've got to get home."

"Melinda, it's still storming out. Why don't you wait a while…or better yet you could stay in my spare room overnight and go home in the morning," Chelsea replied. "I'll even make you breakfast."

"No, I'm good. Thanks for the offer, but I like to sleep in my own bed. Besides, a little rain certainly won't hurt me."

Together the two women walked to the front door. "Oh, wait," Melinda said before Chelsea could unarm the security and open the door. "I have something for you. It's a special gift."

"For me?" Chelsea asked, wondering what Melinda might have for her.

Melinda reached into her oversize bag and withdrew a hatchet. In one quick movement, before Chelsea could absorb what was happening, Melinda swung the hatchet at her, catching her on her upper arm.

The sharpness of the blade sliced through Chelsea's skin. She gasped in pain at the same time she stumbled back from Melinda. "What are you doing?" she screamed. "W-why did you do that?"

Melinda's eyes narrowed, and she took a step toward Chelsea. "Because I want to see you hurt. I want to see you bleed before I kill you."

Chelsea gasped. "Are you crazy? What's wrong with you? Melinda, if this is some sort of a joke, then you need to stop." Chelsea's arm burned as warm blood ran down it. Her breaths came in pants as she looked at her friend in stunned surprise.

"Oh, Chelsea, trust me. This is no joke." Melinda's face twisted into an expression of hatred that Chelsea had never seen before. "You've already escaped me twice, but you won't this time."

Melinda remained several feet away from where Chelsea stood. A new shock raced through Chelsea. Melinda? It had been Melinda who had chased her through the field with the scythe? She was the person who had tried to break into Chelsea's house?

Chelsea's heart raced a million beats a minute. "You? It was all you? But why? Melinda, I'm your friend." Chelsea clasped her hand over her bleeding wound.

"And you totally ruined my life," Melinda screamed, her features displaying a rage Chelsea had never seen before. Melinda raised the hatchet again, and Chelsea took another step backward.

"How did I ruin your life?" Chelsea screamed back, her body poised in fight-or-flight mode.

"By not eating, you stupid bitch. By not taking care of yourself and falling off a damned runway. I had it made in New York. As long as you were doing well, I was living the good life." Melinda's entire body shook with her fury.

"I was living in a great apartment and going to all the A-list parties. I was meeting handsome, sexy men and living the life I deserved, and then you ruined everything. You ruined everything for me!"

"You could have stayed in New York," Chelsea replied fervently.

"What, and gone back to breaking my back working in a deli? No way. You were my ticket to the good life, but without you there was no such thing for me. You ruined it all!" Melinda released a bloodcurdling scream and then rushed toward Chelsea.

Chelsea grabbed the lamp off the end table and threw it at Melinda, but the delicate blingy item merely glanced off her body.

Chelsea frantically looked around for something she could use for her defense. Seeing nothing and with Melinda quickly advancing on her, Chelsea turned and ran to the staircase.

She screamed as Melinda swung the hatchet, barely missing her. The blade hit the wall with a loud thud. "Did you really think I wanted to come back to this stupid little town? Did you really believe I'd be happy marrying some pasty-face farm boy?" The hatchet smashed into the wall again.

Chelsea ran up the stairs as fast as she could, sobs of terror ripping up her throat. She couldn't believe this was happening. She and Melinda had been friends since third grade. How could she come after Chelsea like this now? To add to the madness, the thunder and lightning continued outside as if to match the mayhem that was occurring inside.

Melinda was like a wild animal at her heels. Chelsea screamed as the hatchet caught her in the back of her calf. Thank God it was another glancing blow, but that didn't stop the excruciating pain that roared through her.

Oh, God…oh, God… She had to get someplace safe, but where? She was certain nobody knew Melinda was here. The police weren't going to magically appear to save her. She was all on her own.

She limped as fast as possible and reached the top of the stairs, then whirled around and kicked Melinda as hard as she could in the chest.

The woman reeled backward, flailing her arms for balance. Chelsea hoped Melinda fell, but she didn't stick around to find out. She turned and limped down the hallway.

At least her bedroom door had a lock on it. If she

could just get there, it would buy her some time. Besides, her phone was there. She could call for help.

Her arm screamed with pain, and her leg was pure agony as blood poured out of the wound and onto the wooden floor. Sobs continued to rip through her as her mind tried to grapple with everything that had happened so far.

Melinda really wanted to kill her. It was so hard to believe that she had been the one who had chased Chelsea that night in the field. It was equally difficult to believe it had been Melinda trying to break into her house in the middle of the night with the intention to kill her.

Chelsea felt as if she was in a dream, but there was no waking up from this nightmare. She never suspected that Melinda was her boogeyman, nor had anyone else suspected the woman.

This is happening. This is really happening, a voice screamed inside her head. She wasn't on drugs, and she wasn't crazy. This was real!

Chelsea reached her bedroom and slammed the door shut and locked it. She leaned with her back against it in an effort to catch her breath.

She looked down at her leg. It was still bleeding pretty badly, as was her arm. She squeezed her eyes tightly closed and drew in deep breaths in an effort to get past the pain that seared through her.

"Hey, Chelsea." Melinda's voice came from the other side of the door. "I'm sorry. All this was really meant to be a joke. I never intended to actually hit you with the hatchet. I'm so sorry if I hurt you. I was really just trying to be funny. Why don't you open the door and let me help you clean up your wounds?"

"I don't need your help," Chelsea replied. She knew Melinda was lying. There was no way this was a joke, and there was no way Chelsea was just going to unlock her door and invite the monster into her bedroom. "You're going to need help when the police arrest you," Chelsea added.

Melinda crashed into the door on the other side. "You might as well open the door, Chelsea. There's no place for you to run. There's no place for you to hide. This is really going to happen, Chelsea. You are going to die a grisly, painful death, and I'm going to laugh as I chop you into pieces."

Deep shudders shot up and down Chelsea's body. For a moment she couldn't move, her terror momentarily keeping her frozen in place. Melinda hit the door with so much force the hatchet splintered the wood. Chelsea screamed and moved away from it. Melinda slammed into it again, the blade of the tool breaking through a second time.

Chelsea's mental inertia snapped. She ran to the nightstand where her phone was. She grabbed it and punched Johnny's number. He answered on the first ring, but before she could say anything to him, Melinda hit the door again and Chelsea realized within seconds the enraged Melinda would be inside the bedroom.

And then what? The bathroom off her bedroom didn't have a lock on the door, and in any case that would just prolong the inevitable. She screamed again as the hole in her bedroom door continued to get bigger with each blow Melinda delivered.

Chelsea quickly gazed around the room, seeking a weapon that could counter a hatchet. There was nothing. She was virtually at Melinda's mercy, and the crazed woman had no mercy to give.

Chelsea's gaze shot to the window. Outside the storm still raged, and Melinda was only seconds away from breaking into the bedroom.

Chelsea ran to the window and threw it open. She had two choices. Stay inside and be killed, or take her chances outside.

Stay inside, or go out into a tall tree she had never climbed with lightning striking all around.

New sobs escaped her as she went out the window.

Chapter Twelve

Johnny held his phone in his hand. The call had come from Chelsea, but it must have been a butt-dial, for she wasn't on the phone.

Still, the sounds he heard were hard to discern. There was a loud banging, and as he was trying to figure out what she could be doing at this time of night, he heard her scream. The sound shot chills up his spine.

When she screamed again, utter terror was in the sound. He leaped out of bed. Chelsea was in trouble. The words screamed in his head. He yanked on his jeans and pulled on a white T-shirt. He then grabbed his gun and his truck keys and raced for the door.

Minutes later he was in his truck and headed into town. His heart beat a million beats a minute as a thousand questions whirled in his head.

If somebody had broken in, then why hadn't her security system worked? He hadn't heard an alarm screeching in the phone call. He still had the phone on the call from her, and his phone was on the passenger seat next to him.

He heard another scream, and his blood chilled. Lightning slashed across the sky, followed by a boom of thunder that seemed to shake the very earth.

"You can't escape from me," a voice screamed. "I'm going to chop you into pieces and feed you to the pigs."

That voice… Melinda? Melinda wanted to kill Chelsea? Confusion roared through his head. What the hell was happening? Melinda and Chelsea had been best friends since they were young girls. They had gone to New York together, and Johnny knew from conversations he'd had with Chelsea that she had taken very good care of Melinda once she had started making money.

Thoughts warred in his mind, but at the moment his biggest worry was the fact that he could no longer hear Chelsea. And that scared the hell out of him. What was happening? He had no idea what was going on, but he knew it was vital that he get to her as soon as possible.

Rain pelted his windshield, lowering visibility and slowing his speed. His chest squeezed tight with fear. Whatever was going on, he had to get to Chelsea in time to make sure she wasn't harmed. Any other option was unthinkable.

The rain turned to pebbles of hail, further impeding his speed. Dammit. It was as if the weather was against him…against Chelsea.

He picked up the phone again and still not hearing Chelsea, he made the difficult decision to hang up. He immediately called Lane.

The chief answered on the second ring. "Lane, you need to get to Chelsea's house as soon as possible. She's in danger and needs help right now."

"I'm on my way." Lane disconnected.

Johnny was grateful Lane hadn't hung on the phone asking questions. Right now every second counted. He winced as a lightning flash nearly blinded him.

It was bad enough that Chelsea was afraid of storms, but as he replayed Melinda's words, he couldn't imagine what Chelsea was going through.

Too late. It couldn't be too late. For her…for them. As he reached the town, despite the hail, he increased his speed. He took the corner near Chelsea's house and fishtailed out. He quickly corrected and roared on down the street.

There was no police presence at her house yet. He pulled his truck to a halt in front of her place and then jumped out. The hail changed back to rain, and above the storm sounds, he immediately heard the vague sound of Chelsea screaming.

He raced up to the front door and grabbed the doorknob. It was locked. He cocked his head and listened. It sounded like Chelsea's screams were coming from outside the house. He stepped back, and that's when he saw her.

She was high up in the tree, clinging onto a branch while somebody—he assumed Melinda—slashed out of the window with a hatchet. The wind buffeted the tree, and the branch she clung to swayed back and forth.

Dear God, just looking up to where she was in the tall tree gave him a faint sense of vertigo. "Chelsea," he yelled to be heard above the storm. He quickly wiped a hand down his face as the rain made it difficult for him to see.

A strike of lightning lit up her face as she looked down. He'd never seen such terror. Her features were taut, and her eyes were wide pools of sheer fear. "Johnny," she cried.

"It's okay, baby. I'm here, and I'm not going to allow her to hurt you." But worry shot through him. Where was Melinda now? She had disappeared from the window.

At that same moment, sirens sounded in the distance. The last thing he wanted Chelsea to do was go back in the window of the house where Melinda might be waiting for her.

"Chelsea, honey, can you come down the tree?"

"I can't. Johnny, I'm…I'm too afraid." She screamed as the thunder crashed overhead. She was wound so tight around the tree trunk, it looked as if she was a part of the bark.

Lane's car, followed by two more patrol cars, roared down the street, sirens blaring and lights flashing. As they pulled up in front of Chelsea's house, they cut the sirens.

Lane jumped out of his vehicle and three more officers got out of theirs, and they all ran toward Johnny. "It's Melinda Wells. She tried to kill Chelsea," Johnny said quickly. "I don't know where she is right now. The last I saw, she was inside the house at Chelsea's bedroom window. The front door is locked, and so far, the house alarm hasn't gone off."

The words tumbled from him fast and furiously as he kept his gaze up on Chelsea. "Do you have this handled?" Lane asked as he, too, looked up at Chelsea.

"I'm working on it," Johnny replied.

Chelsea's house alarm began to ring, indicating a breach in the security. "Around back," Lane yelled to his deputies. They all raced around the side of the house, leaving Johnny to try to get Chelsea down from the tree.

The rain had changed to a fine mist, and Johnny was desperate to have Chelsea safe and in his arms. "Chelsea, you can come down now. You're safe."

"Johnny, I'm so afraid. I—I need you to help me." Her words came out with deep sobs.

"Chelsea, pretend you're climbing down the tree to come and meet me at the cabin," he replied.

"I…I can't, Johnny. I really need you to help me down," she cried.

Her need battled with Johnny's fear of heights. Her need of him won out. Thankfully, the tree appeared to be perfect for climbing. "I'm coming, Chelsea," he yelled up and then grabbed a limb and pulled himself up.

As he moved higher in the tree, a sense of dizziness shot off inside him again. When he was halfway up to where she was, he made the mistake of looking down.

His chest tightened, and nausea welled up inside him. He closed his eyes as he clung tight to the tree trunk. The limb beneath his feet swayed with the wind, and he froze.

"Johnny, please help me."

Her voice sliced through his irrational fear. He opened his eyes and looked up. He could do this. He could do this for her. He grabbed the next limb and pulled himself higher.

He continued to climb until he reached the branch just beneath her. It was then he saw the big, bleeding gash in her leg, and any fear he might have entertained about climbing the tree fled beneath his worry for her and a new rage toward Melinda.

"Baby, I'm right here," he said. He needed to get her out of the tree and to the emergency room as soon as possible. The wound in her leg was dripping blood. Who knew how much blood she had already lost?

He stepped up to the limb where she stood and wrapped an arm around her. He realized her arm also had a nasty bleeding wound. Dear God, where else might she be hurt?

"Chelsea, we need to get you down and to the hospital. You can climb down."

"No, I can't," she cried.

"Yes, you can," he countered firmly. "Remember how you used to climb down the tree outside your mother's house to sneak out to see me? This is the same thing. Chelsea, you can climb down this tree with me."

"Okay," she replied tearfully. "With you, Johnny, I can do it."

"Then let's go." He kept his gaze focused on her as he began to work his way back down the tree.

Slowly they climbed down together. The storm was moving out, the thunder more distant than it had been. By the time they reached the ground, Lane was waiting for them. "She must have gone out the back door, but so far, we haven't been able to locate her."

"You take care of getting her in custody. I'm getting Chelsea to the hospital." Johnny didn't wait for a reply. He swept Chelsea up into his arms. Her arms encircled his neck, and she buried her face into his shoulder and began to weep.

He carried her to his truck, opened the door and

gently placed her on the passenger seat. He then closed the door and hurried around to his door.

Before he got there, Chelsea screamed and jerked forward. Melinda hung over the back seat, attempting to grab her. She must have slipped the view of the officers and managed to hide in his truck. Johnny yanked on the driver's-side door. Locked.

He didn't wait for his key to automatically unlock the door, instead he grabbed his gun and swung the butt of it as hard as possible against the window.

The window shattered. He reached in and unlocked the door. Everything only took seconds. Chelsea was screaming and battling with Melinda over the seat.

"Die, you bitch!" Melinda growled and tried to swing her hatchet at Chelsea's head.

Johnny yanked open the back door and reached in and grabbed hold of Melinda. She became a kicking, spitting, scratching hellcat, fighting Johnny to stay in the truck.

"I want her to die," she screamed.

"Not on my watch," Johnny replied. He grabbed the arm with the hatchet and with all his might yanked her out of the truck. He threw her to the ground and then seized the hatchet from her grasp. Lane rushed over to help him, and together they got her to her feet so Lane could handcuff her.

"I'll take her from here," Lane said above Melinda's screams and curses.

Johnny hurried back to his truck where he closed the back door and then got into the driver's seat. Chelsea had quieted. She was no longer screaming or crying. She merely slumped in the seat with her eyes closed. Johnny eyed her worriedly.

"She'll never be able to hurt you again, honey. Lane is taking her straight to jail," he said. Chelsea merely nodded.

He put his truck into Drive and pulled away from the curb. The wounds on her leg and arm were still bleeding, and when he glanced at her, her face was as pale as he'd ever seen it. He suddenly realized she wasn't out of the woods yet. With this frightening thought in mind, he stepped on the gas, frantic to get her to the hospital as quickly as possible.

Minutes later he pulled up in front of the emergency entrance and frantically honked his horn. Two orderlies rushed outside, and Johnny got out. "We need a wheelchair," he cried.

One of the orderlies rushed back toward the hospital and the other one opened the passenger door. Johnny rushed around the truck. "She has a hatchet wound to her leg and arm, and I'm not sure what else."

Chelsea opened her eyes. "Thank you, Johnny. I love you so very much." Her eyes drifted closed again.

For the first time Johnny's abject fear for her roared through his head and heart. He fought back the overwhelming emotions that flooded through him as he helped to get her loaded into the wheelchair.

"I love you too," he shouted as the orderly wheeled her toward the building. "Do you hear me, Chelsea? I love you too."

A sense of helplessness swept through him as he watched them disappear into the hospital. Had he gotten to her in time? The little hospital in Coyote Creek didn't have a specialized trauma unit. Would it have what she needed?

He got back into his truck and pulled it into a regular parking place, then headed to the small emergency waiting room.

Adrienne Alexander was the night receptionist on duty. Johnny checked in with her and then sat in one of the cheap green plastic chairs to wait for a doctor to come out and let him know how Chelsea was doing.

He had so many questions about what had happened. Why had Melinda gone after Chelsea? What might cause a friend to turn into a killing machine? With a hatchet, no less. Once again fear torched through him, tightening his chest and bringing a mist of tears to his eyes.

The minutes ticked by, and the longer it took, the more desperate Johnny felt. What was taking so long? Why hadn't a doctor come out to talk to him yet? Had there been more wounds than had been visible?

Chelsea had to be okay. She just had to be. Their love story couldn't end like this. Not like this with terror and blood and…death.

CHELSEA CAME TO SLOWLY. When she opened her eyes, she immediately knew she was in the hospital, but for several long moments she didn't remember why.

Faint sun crept over the horizon, indicating to her that it was morning. She frowned. Wasn't it storming? She remembered the thunder and lightning.

Then it all slammed back into her brain. The storm…and Melinda. Melinda had tried to kill her. The very idea still didn't seem real.

But it had really happened. She wasn't crazy or on drugs. Melinda had really attacked her with a hatchet. She squeezed her eyes tightly closed. Not only had Melinda hurt her leg and her arm, she'd ripped into Chelsea's very heart.

Melinda had been the friend who had helped Chelsea get through her painful high-school years. She'd been the person who had known all of Chelsea's secrets and desires, and she thought she'd known all of Melinda's too.

But she'd been wrong. She hadn't believed Tanya had an evil soul, yet she had never seen the total rottenness in her own best friend. And it felt like such a deep betrayal.

Her leg ached, as did her arm. She raised her arm up to look at the area where Melinda had sliced her, but it was covered in a long bandage.

Her thoughts were all scattered. She hoped Melinda went to prison for a very long time. Chelsea certainly never wanted to see the woman again. She also hoped she never found herself in the top of a tree during a thunderstorm again. As she remembered the booming, deafening thunder and the sizzle of nearby lightning, a chill shot through her body.

The chill immediately warmed. Johnny had climbed the tree for her. The awe of that moment sat with her and brought with it a wave of warmth.

She knew how frightened he was of heights. He'd been scared of heights since he was a kid. Yet somehow he'd managed to set that aside and climb up a tree to help her get down.

Her heart swelled with love for him. Thank God he'd arrived last night when he had. Thank God the police had shown up when they had. If nobody had come in time…she'd be dead right now.

She'd love to see Johnny, but she knew he'd have chores to do. He knew she was safe, and he'd probably come to see her sometime this afternoon.

With that thought in mind, she drifted back to sleep. About an hour later she was awakened by Carrie Carlson, a cute young nurse with dark hair and blue-violet eyes. "I'm sorry to wake you," she said to Chelsea. "I need to take your vitals."

"It's okay. I was ready to wake up anyway."

"Let me get your temperature first."

Carrie quickly went through her routine and then smiled with a gentleness at Chelsea. "How are you feeling this morning?"

"Good, except for the pain in my arm and leg," Chelsea admitted.

"On a scale of one to ten, ten being the worse pain you've ever had, where are you?" Carrie asked.

Chelsea frowned. "Maybe about a seven."

"I'll speak to the doctor about giving you some pain medication. In any case, he should be in to speak to you in just a little while."

"Thanks," Chelsea replied.

Minutes later Carrie was back with pain meds that she put into Chelsea's IV, and some minutes after that, Chelsea dozed off.

She was awakened by the doctor coming in. She was pleased to see it was Dr. Michael Morris. The gray-haired man with his warm brown eyes had been Chelsea's doctor through most of her life.

"Chelsea, how are you feeling this morning?" he asked.

"Better now that I got a little pain medication in me," she replied. "So, tell me the damage."

"I don't know how much you remember from last night when you were brought in. You were in shock and had lost a lot of blood, and then there were the wounds on your arm and leg."

He paused and pulled a chair up closer to her bed and sat. His eyes emoted great empathy. "The first thing we did was give you a tetanus shot. Your arm took twenty-two stitches. Thankfully it appeared to be a glancing wound that didn't go into any muscle or nerves beneath the skin."

She winced. "And what about my leg?"

"Unfortunately, that was a little more complicated. We had to do some internal stitching as the wound was deeper. Externally you have fifty-four stitches. I tried to do them small and neat, hoping the scar you'll have won't look too bad. But it will be significant."

"I'm alive, and that's all I really care about. When can I bust out of this joint?"

"I'm pumping you full of good antibiotics today. As long as your vitals stay fine, you could possibly go home later this afternoon."

"That would be terrific," she replied.

However, as the hours went by, the idea of going back to her house grew more and more repugnant. She knew there was damage to the wall going up the stairs, and her bedroom door was smashed to pieces.

Everywhere she looked in the house there would be memories of a madwoman chasing her with a hatchet in an effort to kill her. Hopefully those memories would fade once the damage was repaired and some time had passed.

She dozed off again, and this time when she

opened her eyes, Johnny was in the chair next to her bed. As she gazed at him, all the horrifying emotions from the night before rose up inside her.

Chapter Thirteen

Johnny saw the wealth of emotions that crossed Chelsea's features, and the fear and the pain as her eyes misted with tears and her lower lip began to tremble.

Before he could respond to her she laughed, and the tears in her eyes disappeared instead of running down her cheeks. "Johnny, you climbed a tree for me," she said.

He smiled at her. "I did, although don't think I'm going to do that all the time now."

Her smile immediately faltered and shadows darkened her eyes. "I hope you never, ever have to do that again for me."

He reached out and took her hand in his. "How are you feeling? Are you in a lot of pain?"

"The pain isn't too bad right now. They gave me some medication a while ago, and it took the edge off it. Have you talked to Dr. Morris?"

"I spoke to him just a few minutes ago. He's writing up the orders to let you go. Are you ready to go home?"

She hesitated several long moments and then nodded. "Sure, I'm ready."

However, it was obvious by her hesitation that she wasn't. "Are you wanting to stay here longer, maybe so they can continue to ease your pain with meds?"

She drew in a deep breath and released it on a shuddery sigh. "No, it's not that. I know my leg and my arm are going to hurt, and I can handle the pain. It's just that…that…the house… She destroyed it, Johnny."

"I was actually going to suggest that you come home with me, and tomorrow we can get Jeb to work on fixing what she wrecked," he said.

"Really? Are you sure you wouldn't mind?" Her eyes instantly brightened at his suggestion.

He squeezed her hand tightly. "Chelsea, I promise you I won't mind. I'd love to have you stay with me. Besides, it's doctor's orders. He doesn't want you up and around on that leg for a while."

She frowned. "We'll need to go by my house and get some clothes and things."

"I'll let Lane know because I imagine your house is a crime scene right now. Has he been here to talk to you yet?"

She shook her head. "I haven't spoken to anyone today except the doctor and a couple of the nurses."

Johnny knew sooner or later Lane would need to

get a statement from her, and he knew that would be difficult for her. If he had his way, he would take her memories of Melinda and the night before away from her and put them someplace where they couldn't hurt her ever again.

He'd wanted to be here first thing this morning, but when he'd called the doctor for an update, he'd indicated that she was sleeping. Not wanting to interfere with her getting her rest, he'd waited until now to come to see her.

And he was ready to take her home with him.

His sleep had been haunted by terrible nightmares. They had been dreams where Melinda had killed Chelsea and he'd watched, frozen in place and unable to do anything about it. That nightmare had ended only for another one to unfold. In that one, Chelsea was up in the tree and couldn't get down. The lightning hit all around the tree, and Johnny knew it was just a matter of time before a killer electrical current zapped through the tree…and Chelsea. Yet he couldn't climb the tree to help her down.

All he wanted to do tonight was hold her in his arms to assure himself she was really and truly okay. "Johnny, I can't tell you how much I love you," she now said.

Before he could reply, the nurse walked in. He recognized her as Emily Timmons, who they had both gone to high school with.

"Hi, Chelsea, Johnny," she said with a bright

smile. "I'm here to get you out of this place," she said to the patient.

"That sounds good to me," Chelsea replied.

Johnny released her hand as Emily set up a tray and grabbed fresh bandages from a shelf. "The first thing I'm going to do is remove your IV," Emily said. It took her only moments to get rid of the line.

"And now I'm going to change your bandages so you go home with clean ones," Emily continued. Carefully, she removed the one on Chelsea's arm.

When Johnny saw the row of stitches, his stomach tightened. Melinda was lucky to be in Lane's custody. Otherwise, Johnny didn't know what he might have done to the woman.

Emily changed the bandage and then moved down to take care of Chelsea's leg. When she exposed the long line of stitches, Johnny once again felt a rage directed at the woman who had attacked Chelsea.

This wound was much bigger…much uglier than the one on her arm. It was obvious from Chelsea's stunned look at it that this was the first time she'd seen it.

Tears sprang to her eyes, but she quickly swiped them away and then released a shaky laugh. "Well, I guess it's official. There's definitely no more modeling in my future."

Her words chilled a place deep in Johnny's heart. He didn't want Chelsea by default. He didn't want her to choose him because her option of returning to modeling was over. He wanted her to choose him because she loved him more than modeling and more than the spotlight and city life. He wanted her to want him more than anything else, and now he wouldn't know if he was really just her second choice for happiness.

She was finally bandaged up and had a prescription for pain pills in her hand, and Emily helped her into a wheelchair. She was going home in the nightgown she'd been wearing the night before. "I'll go ahead and pull my truck up out front," Johnny said.

He hurried out of the hospital and to his truck. The early evening was clear with no signs of the storm that had blown through the night before.

Last night he'd been ready to ask her again to marry him. He'd been ready to give the ring back to her. But now, he felt himself mentally taking a step back from her.

She definitely would need help through her recuperation. Her doctor's orders had been for her to stay off her feet for a couple of weeks. He certainly intended to be here for her while she got better, and in that time he needed to figure out if they were really meant to be together forever.

Once Chelsea was settled into his truck, he made a stop to pick up her pain meds, and then they stopped at her place where Lane allowed him to go in and get some clothes for her. By the time they arrived at the cabin, he could tell that she was hurting and tired.

He picked her up and carried her into the cabin and gently placed her on the sofa. "Sit tight, and I'll get you a blanket and a pain tablet."

"Thank you, Johnny. I don't know what I'd do without you," she replied with a tired smile.

"Right now you don't have to know," he replied.

Minutes later she was snuggled beneath a soft blanket, and Johnny sat in his recliner and watched her sleep. His love for her nearly overwhelmed him. He'd loved her since he was seventeen. He didn't know how to love anyone else. He'd never really wanted to love anyone else. She was in his heart and in his very soul.

The question was: Did she love him in the same way, or was he her second choice? Was she now defaulting to him because, as she said, modeling was now out of the question?

CHELSEA HAD BEEN at Johnny's place for almost a week. The day after she'd come here she'd set Jeb to work on repairing the damage to her house, but what she really wanted was for Johnny to tell her to sell the place and make a forever home here with him at the cabin.

However, she felt a distance from him, a strange detachment that had her feeling less confident of where their relationship was going. Each night she slept in his arms, in his bed under the stars. He'd made no attempt to make love to her, and she was beginning to wonder if his love for her had somehow changed.

Had the craziness and drama of Melinda put him off? Lane had come by on her second day at Johnny's to get her statement. Johnny had sat next to her as she'd relived the horror of that night. But was he over it? Was he over her?

Each morning he made sure she'd eaten breakfast and had everything she might need at her fingertips before he left for work. He stopped and checked in with her at noon and then returned for the day at around six.

She was now seated in the kitchen, waiting for his arrival home. She usually sat there and watched him make dinner, and he talked about things around the ranch, and she caught him up on what television shows she'd watched during the day.

Ashley had been very supportive and understanding about her not working in the store until the doctor completely released Chelsea and she was feeling better. Ashley had promised Chelsea that the job would still be hers when she was ready.

She now looked up with a smile as Johnny came in through the back door. "Hey, handsome," she said.

He flashed her a quick smile. "Hey, beautiful," he replied. "How was your day?"

"Fine, although I can't wait to get all these stitches out. They're starting to itch."

"Right now, those stitches are holding you together. Don't hurry the healing process." He walked over to the sink and washed his hands, then moved to the refrigerator and took out a package of hamburger. "I figured I'd fry us up a couple of burgers for dinner."

"Sounds good to me. Once I get these stitches out I can start cooking meals for you. Of course, once I get better, I'll be back at my own place."

She waited for him to protest her words. She waited for him to tell her that he wanted her here in the cabin with him forever. When that didn't happen a wave of apprehension shot through her.

She'd thought they were on the same page, that they were building a stronger, deeper relationship with each day that passed and that very quickly she'd be by his side every day and every night.

"Johnny, is everything all right?" she asked once he had the hamburger patties in the skillet.

"Sure. Why do you ask?" He sat in the chair across from her.

"You've just felt a little distant since I've been here." She searched his features. "I know it's been difficult to take care of me along with everything else you have on your plate."

He flashed her a quick smile. "Taking care of you is the least of my problems."

"What can I do to help with the other problems?" she asked.

"If you could catch the person who murdered my father, that would go a long way in solving some of the other issues."

"Oh, Johnny." She covered one of his hands with hers. "I wish I could do that for you."

He turned his hand over so he held hers, and for a long moment their gazes locked. Myriad emotions chased across the blue depths of his…sadness and a touch of anger and something else…something she couldn't quite identify.

He pulled his hand away and stood. "I need to flip these burgers."

She watched as he took care of the cooking and then pulled out a fat tomato, a head of lettuce and several slices of cheese from the fridge.

"Can I help?" she asked.

"No, I've got this."

He said no more as he finished preparing the evening meal. As they ate, she tried to make conversation with him, but he remained quiet and obviously distant.

It scared her. Was he having doubts where she was concerned? Did he see her now as damaged goods? Was his love for her waning? She'd always wanted to be Johnny's girl. She'd wanted to be his forever girl, and she'd thought that was what he wanted too. Now she wasn't so sure anymore.

It was a quiet meal, and when it was finished while he cleared the dishes she went back to the sofa. She'd felt like having a second chance with Johnny had been a gift from Heaven, but now she wasn't so sure. Maybe fate had only been laughing at her.

Johnny came into the living room and sat in his chair, although he didn't recline it. Instead, he once again held her gaze for a long moment.

"Chelsea, I've been doing a lot of thinking over the past few days," he said.

"Thinking about what?" She tried to read him, but his features gave nothing away.

"About us."

Her stomach churned with tension, and her heart began to race. "What about us?"

"I wasn't sure I wanted to be your default. I didn't want to be the one you chose because your injury took modeling away from you, but I've realized now I'll take you however I can get you."

To her surprise, he fell to one knee and pulled the ring he'd given her once before out of his pocket. "Will you marry me, Chelsea? Will you marry me and make me the happiest man on the face of the earth?"

Her initial joy was tempered by his words. "Johnny, you aren't my default. I'm not choosing you because modeling is now out of the question. It was out of the question the moment you told me you wanted to try again with me."

She got up from the sofa, took his hand and tugged him to his feet. "Johnny, I love you. You're my first choice in love. There has never been anything or anyone I love more than you."

His features relaxed and softened, and his eyes gazed at her with the love that had always made her feel as if she was home. She wound her arms around his neck. "Johnny, I thought I lost you once, and I never want to lose you again. Yes, I'll marry you, and that would have been my answer if you'd asked me before I got all these stitches."

She might have said more, but at that moment his lips took hers in a kiss that spoke of love and passion and commitment. When the kiss stopped, he slid the ring on her finger.

"I've loved you forever, Chelsea, and I will continue to love you through eternity. I want to marry you and have babies with you and build our lives here together." His eyes, those beautiful eyes of his, gazed at her with love.

This was really happening. She wasn't crazy and she wasn't on drugs. This beautiful moment with Johnny was really happening, and a voice whispered happiness into her heart.

"Yes, please." She looked up at him with all the love she had in her heart. "When can we start?"

He laughed. "We might have to wait a little bit for our wedding, but we can start making babies as soon as you feel better."

"I'm feeling better right now," she replied half-breathlessly.

Without warning he scooped her up in his arms and carried her toward the bedroom. But she knew he was carrying her to her future.

She knew with her Johnny it was going to be a future filled with laughter and passion and ever-lasting love.

Epilogue

Johnny stepped out of the cabin and into the waning light of day. Chelsea was sleeping in his bed with his ring on her finger, and for the moment a wealth of happiness filled his heart.

The girl he'd grown up loving was the woman he would love until the end of time. He knew she felt the same way. He refused to allow any doubts about her loving him to enter his mind. He'd decided in the past three days that even if he only had her in his life for a day or a month it was worth it.

However, he knew in his heart they were going to be together forever. He'd known it since he'd been a boy. She was his person, and he knew he was hers.

She was going to be the mother of his children, and he knew she'd be awesome at the job. He couldn't wait to start building a family with her.

He looked in the distance and frowned as he saw Leroy and Caleb outside the barn. He still believed his brother and the ranch hand had secrets. He just didn't know if their secrets had anything to do with his father's murder.

Then there was his worry about Luke. His younger brother seemed to be holding on to his sanity by a thread, and Johnny feared what might happen if that connection broke.

Finally, there was the fact that nobody had been arrested for his father's murder. Lane had admitted to him earlier that day that the case had gone completely cold, and he had no real suspect in mind.

Johnny couldn't stand the fact that his dad's murderer was walking around free in town. He hoped like hell Caleb had nothing to do with their father's death and that he could find a way to walk Luke through his anger and grief. Only time would tell.

In the meantime, he had a warm, loving woman in his bed, and the stars had begun to shine overhead. It was time for Johnny to get into bed and enjoy both of those things.

* * * * *

Don't miss the next suspenseful tale in the Kings of Coyote Creek miniseries. And be sure to pick up other exciting stories from Carla Cassidy:

Deadly Days of Christmas
Stalker in the Shadows
Stalked in the Night
48 Hour Lockdown

Available from Harlequin Intrigue!

WE HOPE YOU ENJOYED
THIS BOOK FROM
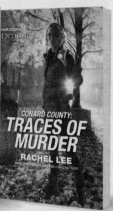 HARLEQUIN
INTRIGUE

Seek thrills. Solve crimes. Justice served.

Dive into action-packed stories that will keep you
on the edge of your seat. Solve the crime
and deliver justice at all costs.

6 NEW BOOKS AVAILABLE EVERY MONTH!

His hands cupped her face. She blinked up at him.

"They buried me," she said, fighting the emotion
trying to take over at the thought of never seeing him
again.

Anger flashed in his blue eyes, and his jaw muscles
clenched. "They better never touch you again. We can
make an excuse to get you out of here. Say one of your
family members is sick and you had to go."

"They'll see it as weakness," she reminded him. "It'll
hurt the case."

He thumbed a loose tendril of hair off her face.

"I don't care, Ree," he said with an overwhelming
intensity that became its own physical presence. "I can't
lose you."

Those words hit her with the force of a tsunami.

Neither of them could predict what would happen next. Neither could guarantee this case wouldn't go south. Neither could guarantee they would both walk away in one piece.

"Let's take ourselves off the case together," she said, knowing full well he wouldn't take her up on the offer but suggesting it anyway.

Quint didn't respond. When she pulled back and looked into his eyes, she understood why. A storm brewed behind those sapphire-blues, crystalizing them, sending fiery streaks to contrast against the whites. Those babies were the equivalent of a raging wildfire that would be impossible to put out or contain. People said eyes were the window to the soul. In Quint's case, they seemed the window to his heart.

He pressed his forehead against hers and took in an audible breath. When he exhaled, it was like he was releasing all his pent-up frustration and fear. In that moment, she understood the gravity of what he'd been going through while she'd been gone. Kidnapped. For all he knew, left for dead.

So she didn't speak, either. Instead, she leaned into their connection, a connection that tethered them as an electrical current ran through her to him and back. For a split second, it was impossible to determine where he ended and she began.

Don't miss
Mission Honeymoon *by Barb Han,*
available August 2022 wherever
Harlequin Intrigue books and ebooks are sold.

Harlequin.com

Get 4 FREE REWARDS!

We'll send you 2 FREE Books plus 2 FREE Mystery Gifts.

FREE Value Over **$20**

Both the **Harlequin Intrigue®** and **Harlequin® Romantic Suspense** series feature compelling novels filled with heart-racing action-packed romance that will keep you on the edge of your seat.

YES! Please send me 2 FREE novels from the Harlequin Intrigue or Harlequin Romantic Suspense series and my 2 FREE gifts (gifts are worth about $10 retail). After receiving them, if I don't wish to receive any more books, I can return the shipping statement marked "cancel." If I don't cancel, I will receive 6 brand-new Harlequin Intrigue Larger-Print books every month and be billed just $5.99 each in the U.S. or $6.49 each in Canada, a savings of at least 14% off the cover price or 4 brand-new Harlequin Romantic Suspense books every month and be billed just $4.99 each in the U.S. or $5.74 each in Canada, a savings of at least 13% off the cover price. It's quite a bargain! Shipping and handling is just 50¢ per book in the U.S. and $1.25 per book in Canada.* I understand that accepting the 2 free books and gifts places me under no obligation to buy anything. I can always return a shipment and cancel at any time. The free books and gifts are mine to keep no matter what I decide.

Choose one: ☐ **Harlequin Intrigue Larger-Print** (199/399 HDN GNXC)   ☐ **Harlequin Romantic Suspense** (240/340 HDN GNMZ)

Name (please print)

Address   Apt. #

City   State/Province   Zip/Postal Code

Email: Please check this box ☐ if you would like to receive newsletters and promotional emails from Harlequin Enterprises ULC and its affiliates. You can unsubscribe anytime.

Mail to the Harlequin Reader Service:
IN U.S.A.: P.O. Box 1341, Buffalo, NY 14240-8531
IN CANADA: P.O. Box 603, Fort Erie, Ontario L2A 5X3

Want to try 2 free books from another series! Call 1-800-873-8635 or visit www.ReaderService.com.

---

*Terms and prices subject to change without notice. Prices do not include sales taxes, which will be charged (if applicable) based on your state or country of residence. Canadian residents will be charged applicable taxes. Offer not valid in Quebec. This offer is limited to one order per household. Books received may not be as shown. Not valid for current subscribers to the Harlequin Intrigue or Harlequin Romantic Suspense series. All orders subject to approval. Credit or debit balances in a customer's account(s) may be offset by any other outstanding balance owed by or to the customer. Please allow 4 to 6 weeks for delivery. Offer available while quantities last.

Your Privacy—Your information is being collected by Harlequin Enterprises ULC, operating as Harlequin Reader Service. For a complete summary of the information we collect, how we use this information and to whom it is disclosed, please visit our privacy notice located at corporate.harlequin.com/privacy-notice. From time to time we may also exchange your personal information with reputable third parties. If you wish to opt out of this sharing of your personal information, please visit readerservice.com/consumerschoice or call 1-800-873-8635. **Notice to California Residents**—Under California law, you have specific rights to control and access your data. For more information on these rights and how to exercise them, visit corporate.harlequin.com/california-privacy.

HIHRS22